Wednesday's Child
& Other Stories

Wednesday's Child
& Other Stories

NISHA SHANKAR

PARTRIDGE
A Penguin Random House Company

To order additional copies of this book, contact
Partridge India
000 800 10062 62
orders.india@partridgepublishing.com

www.partridgepublishing.com/india

Dedicated to my father. Love you appa...

PROLOGUE

Caroline Winters rode her tricycle slowly around the house. It was mid June and the day was cool. There was no wind and the leaves on the trees were completely still. It was going to be another long and uneventful day. Her curly auburn hair felt damp after her bath and stuck to the back of her neck. She shivered slightly in the cold. She was an attractive child with milk white skin and huge eyes the colour of a storm tossed sea, that were set wide apart. Her tiny mouth formed an 'o' as she blew out a gust of air which came out as a puff of smoke. She squinted her eyes as she tried looking up at the sky. The weather was unseasonably cool and the sky was an ominous gray.

She could see her neighbour, old Mrs Brent pottering around in her garden. She was attempting to trim a few plants near the porch. Other than her, there was absolutely no one she could see. Caroline began yet another revolution in her garden. Her mother and daddy had gone to meet granny. She had wanted to go too but Daddy said "Next time sweetheart" absently and he and mommy left soon after. Her sitter Beth was supposed to be minding her but she could see her through the glass of the patio doors, stretched out on the couch with the ever present phone stuck in her ear. Beth acted responsible only when her parents were around. At all other times she was either talking on the phone or lazing in front of the TV with a bag of popcorn.

Caroline didn't like Beth but when mommy was away, she was the one she was stuck with, the only person who could understand her. She had tried signalling to Beth that she wanted to go out and play but Beth had ignored her. She tried tugging at Beth's skirt, but Beth shook her head, rolled her eyes and continued her conversation on the phone.

Caroline sighed and went out by herself. Mommy had strictly forbidden her to go out of the house alone ever and so she played by herself in the garden. She was near the gate when she saw a couple standing in front of their car. The hood of the car was open and was sending out a lot of smoke. She strained to have a closer look without going out. The woman stood with her back to Caroline, her hands on her hips. She was wearing a maroon top with a beige skirt. It wasn't pretty, not like the clothes mommy wore. Her waist length hair was tawny which she wore in a straggly pony tail.

The man kept blowing out gusts of air and rubbing his hands while bending and peering in front of the car. Something about his face and stance frightened Caroline. He was big and burly with massive arms and a mean looking face. He appeared to be tinkering with the front of the car. She did not know for how long she actually stood there but when looked around she suddenly found that it was beginning to get dark. Mrs Brent had long since gone back into her house and there was no one on the street. She was surprised to find that in her curiosity, she had actually come out of her house and onto the street. The man looked up suddenly and their eyes locked together. The fear that gripped her was so sudden that she was momentarily paralysed. She turned to run towards her house the man caught her proceeded to pin her arms against her body. As she opened her mouth in a soundless gasp she felt a cloth being shoved on her face. Her first instinct was to inhale and almost immediately afterward she felt herself beginning to get drowsy. They shoved her in the car and her last thought before she plunged into darkness was that Mommy had warned her not to go outside alone.

CHAPTER 1

Detectives Andrew Morgan and Scott Brennan sat in the back of the car while detective Raglan drove. They were heading from Nicollet Avenue to Glenwood Avenue, where the kidnapping had been called in. The estimated time to get there was 13 minutes and they had just started. Paula Seaver sat next to Bill Raglan staring forward as the car made its way to the Winters' home.

"What have we got?" Det Morgan's question cut through the noise of the traffic like lightning. The surprising thing about his voice was that it was quite low but could be heard even in a very high noise environment without any effort on the part of the listener. Paula began filling him in on the details they'd received. "Vic is a 6 year old by the name of Caroline Winters. She'd supposedly been outside playing in the garden alone when the kidnapping had happened. No witnesses have come forward with any helpful information as yet and no demand has been made".

"Parents? Sitter? Anyone?" This typically was from Brennan. Lt Brennan of the police squad headed this team. He had the habit of coming right to the point with the minimum of fuss. His manner of speaking was one which people found disconcertingly cold. But people who knew him well understood the reason for the lack of eloquence. In his job, any kind of delay could get people killed. It was not for nothing that he made the transition from rookie cop to lieutenant pretty early in his career.

"The sitter was supposed to be minding the kid", Paula's tone implied that they had not managed to obtain any more information about that. Morgan grunted. "You'd think that with the number of kids going missing everyday, parents would know more than to leave their child with an irresponsible teenager". He opened his mouth to continue when Raglan cut in with "A child gets kidnapped at approximately once every 40 seconds in the US which works out to about 2000 a day. Of the 800000 missing in a year around 69000 are abducted. The average non family perpetrator in these cases is generally male".

All of this was delivered in 5 seconds in the same monotone. This was the kind of conversation Raglan made. An autodidact, Raglan was the most knowledgeable person in the team. The standing joke at the precinct was that Raglan had more number of PhDs than everyone else in the department put together. He had had an abusive childhood which was why he had decided to turn his life around by pursuing a career in the police force. Earlier he had been diagnosed with 'Asperger's Syndrome'. That essentially meant that while his cognitive skills were intact, maybe even enhanced, his social skills were practically non-existent. But he was invaluable to their team as his extensive knowledge on criminology helped them nab their victims time and again. After he had become part of their team his communication skills had marginally improved and he stopped taking what everyone said literally and made an attempt to comprehend the difference between jokes and serious talk.

"It's that house there". Paula motioned for Raglan to stop. The house had a couple of squad cars parked in front and the place was evidently in a flurry of activity. As the team headed inside, Morgan looked around and made a note of everything around him. He had a photographic memory which as a cop he both blessed and cursed. While the fact that he never forgot the details of a crime scene meant that his memory was invaluable to help solve a case, it also obviously meant that he never forgot the gory images which impressed themselves on his subconscious and were the cause for several recurrent nightmares. Nothing here seemed unusual however.

They made their way to the living room where they could see the parents huddled together on the couch. The mother was sobbing unrestrainedly while the father's grief seemed beyond tears. Morgan also noted a teenager, presumably the sitter who stood to one side, futilely dabbing at her eyes with a tissue. Standing next to her was middle aged woman with a worn face. A gamut of emotions was crossing her face. He could make out sadness, pity, fear and something else he couldn't quite describe at first... Defiance? Then seeing her wrap her arm protectively around the sitter's shoulder he understood. That was the mother.

Seaver was going to have her work cut out for her. The youngest in the team and the most effective in terms of communication and gisting the data obtained from the family and friends of the victim, she was nicknamed 'The Interface'.

Her sympathetic tone and the genuine concern reflected in her eyes made them unburden their feelings to her completely.

The sitter's mother caught his eye and the thin lines of her mouth tightened as though daring him to question her daughter. This was undoubtedly going to be one hell of an investigation he thought wryly.

CHAPTER 2

She was in a boat. She felt herself moving side to side like when she had gone fishing with daddy last year. The boat had rocked a lot and her tummy had begun to feel weird. It was like that now except... Everything was dark... She opened her eyes... Everything was still dark. She remembered she was in a car. She could feel her hands behind her back. Her wrists felt so sore. She realized that she had been tied up. The ropes were knotted too tight. Her legs hurt so much. Her head was still covered. The cloth felt rough and scratchy against her face. It smelled really bad. She felt like she was going to puke. She forced herself to think of mommy. How pretty she always looked. How much she loved her. Thinking about that made her want to cry. She could feel it welling up inside her throat, choking her, making it hard to breathe.

Before she could do anything else she felt the car jerk to a stop. The sudden movement made her roll onto her back. The pain in her hands shot up and she felt momentarily dizzy. She could feel the car tremor as someone got out and shut the door hard.

She felt air rush in suddenly and realized that someone had yanked open the boot of the car. Instinctively she shrank back. Hard, strong arms picked her up roughly and began walking. The next thing she knew was that someone had dropped her on something soft. She felt the man's hands tug the sack off her face. She blinked hard, her eyes attempting to adjust to the sudden blaze of light. As her eyes adjusted she saw that the blaze of light was nothing more than a rusty bulb right over her head which gave off a flickering yellow light.

The man appeared to be saying something to her. She shook her head and tried to push herself back. This appeared to make him angry. He turned to the side and said something. The woman appeared. The look on her face frightened Caroline even more. She instinctively sensed that the woman was afraid of the man. The woman said something to the man which apparently brought on an argument. Suddenly the man bent down and untied her wrists. He was asking her something again. She saw his neck redden as he yelled at her. Flecks of spittle hit her face as he pushed his face closer to her and said something. She flinched as though he had hit her.

In a frightened movement she thrust her arms in front of her face. The movement seemed to throw him a bit. She motioned to him that she was unable to hear or speak. His eyes widened and he stepped back. He walked deliberately over to the woman and slapped her hard across her face. And then everything went dark.

CHAPTER 3

"What did I tell you Sarah?"... "What have you done?" he asked quietly. His voice escalated exponentially in volume. "What in hell did I tell you and what have you done you moron? Why didn't you tell me that the old hag may have been at the window?". He had a tendency to repeat himself in times of anger and stress. Living with him for seven years had made her painfully aware of just how unstable Alex was. His mood swings were dramatic and extreme and of late, he had been continually mad. Earlier she would have tried to stand up to him and fight but now she knew him too well to attempt anything so stupid.

The corner of her mouth was bleeding, but she made no attempt to stem the flow fearing that the movement would infuriate him further. Every minute of every day made her curse the instinct that had made her marry Alex Osborne. The fact that he was a psychopath somehow had escaped her then. The realization came too late. She remembered how her mom had discouraged her from getting involved with him. But her mom was pessimistic most of the time.

Ironically, it was to get away from her mother that she had rushed into marriage.

She snapped out of these thoughts as she realized he was watching her. He was sore about the kid being dumb and he was going to take it out on her, she knew. "You really hate me for making you do this, don't you?". She saw the murderous rage begin to build in his eyes again. It was uncanny how he managed to guess what she was thinking most of the time. "Nno-no Alex.. Of course not." She managed to stammer.

But of course she didn't fool him. His face narrowed into a sneer. "What a pathetic creature you are! No guts, no backbone! Yyyesss Alex, Nnnoo Alex, wwhatever you sssay Alex! You dumb sissy! You're a moron! You hear me? A moron! Do you realize we may have been spotted?". He was goading her, she knew. But she had no intention of letting him get under her skin. Long ago she had learnt not to rise to his bait because the repercussions were severe. Once in an unusual display of courage she'd fought back. He'd slammed her face into the sink so hard that her cheek bone cracked and two of her teeth fell out. The laceration was so deep that she'd had to have 12 stitches and it had left an ugly scar along the side of her face. When she'd got her face bandaged, she lied to the doctor and told him that she'd slipped on the stairs. His incredulous look of complete disbelief had discouraged further conversation. Over the years she'd been hit too many times to count. The thought of going to the police never entered her mind and if it did she certainly never acted on it.

She never knew when he'd get the urge to pick up a kid. It always happened when they were cruising along the road in their car. His secret was that though he knew exactly 'what' to do, the 'when' was left to fate. Targets were random but always girls, all red heads and always between the ages of 4 and 7. The decision to choose a particular kid was always impulsive. Incredibly, over the years he'd been able to pull off as many as 20 kidnappings and no one had the slightest clue who was responsible. Every time he'd been able to lure the kids by piquing their curiosity. A couple of times he'd pulled the smoke act. The smoke was nothing but a couple of bags of dry ice which he unobtrusively placed in front of the car so the kids couldn't see. In any case a kid that young wasn't smart enough to know the difference.

The obvious problem in this method was that they might be spotted by someone like a neighbour. She was supposed to be the look out. The first few times he hadn't trusted her and done everything himself, but then seeing that she never put up any kind of resistance to anything he did, he got a perverse pleasure in including her in his plans, knowing that she hated doing it. She hated the whole thing. She'd kept a look out today as well. Just as they were driving away however Alex fancied that he saw the old woman across the street at her window. He was getting paranoid these days. It made her life if possible even more unendurable. *I just hope this paranoia kills him* she thought vengefully.

They'd never had any kids of their own. At first she'd been disappointed, even ashamed. When the abductions began she even thought that he did them out of a longing to have children. Until the first one died. She never forgot the way he'd looked that night. Completely crazy. The memory of it still paralysed her with fear.

They all died. Every single one of them. He couldn't deal with kids. They all failed him, one way or another and when that happened, they were on a one way ride out of earth. She'd given up wondering whether his obsession would ever stop. He was a madman. She knew that now. The only way to avoid a certain and painful death would be to do as she was told. Like her mother used to tell her when she was young "Get this straight hon. To stay outta trouble means to do as your told".

CHAPTER 4

Paula sat across the couch and looked at Myra Winters compassionately. She couldn't have been more than 28 or 29. Her face showed so much fear and grief for her child. Next to her sat her husband whose face looked like it was carved of wood.

"Ma'am, I know what you are going through. It must be a very difficult time for you, but it is important that you answer my questions." *God knows how many times I've repeated this* she thought. It certainly didn't make it easier with time.

She saw Myra make an effort to stop weeping and look up at her. "Yes". Her voice was low and measured and showed a lot of strain. It was obvious that she had to exercise immense self control to answer her.

"Your daughter is six years old. Is that right?". Too overwhelmed to speak, Myra nodded.

"I'm going to need a picture and some other details as well. Try to be positive ma'am, kids these days are pretty smart. Your daughter may be able to communicate with someone."

"You don't understand!" Myra burst out passionately, "my daughter is incapable of speech and she is deaf!". She broke down completely.

Shit! Paula thought to herself *how on earth did we miss this?.* This unexpected piece of information had just made their case a thousand times more difficult. *How many children have I managed to return to their parents in my entire career?* she reflected, *maybe three or four at best and none of them had had deaf mutism.* She remembered one of her cop pals tell her that once when they had to deal with the kidnapping of a deaf child, the child had been found mutilated beyond recognition. Even the mother couldn't recognise her. Only conclusive DNA evidence had led them to determine who the child was. She consciously put that disquieting thought out of her mind.

"We're gonna need to compile a list of all the possible suspects" she told her colleagues. "We need you to give us a clear picture of what you think happened" she told Myra gently. "We also need a picture of Caroline". Charles Winters went over to the chest on the side of the room and brought out a picture of the child. "This was taken about a month earlier" he whispered, his voice choking with emotion.

My God thought Paula as she looked at the photograph. Caroline appeared to be sitting on a tricycle and had clearly been caught unawares when the picture was taken. Even so, Paula could see that the child was exceptionally beautiful. She shuddered thinking of the child being in the hands of an abusive kidnapper. She turned to the mother. "So tell me what happened"

Myra controlled herself as best she could and began. "Charles and I had to go out. We don't usually go out without her, Caro...." This brought on a fresh lot of tears. Making an obvious effort, she continued, "This was an absolute necessity. Charles' mother was ill and admitted in the hospital. We had to go see her. We did not want Caro to come along because we did not want her to see her grandma like that. She loves her and the sight of her grandma looking so sick and ill would have scared her. Oh, I wish we'd taken her now!". She lapsed into sobs again.

Paula noticed a movement at the corner of her eye. It was the sitter and she appeared to be crying silently. As she looked at the wretched girl, she felt a slight sense of pity pervade her. The girl really was filled with remorse. She glanced at Brennan and with a slight movement of her head indicated that he take over the questioning of Myra. She turned back to Myra. "Lt. Brennan will take it from here" she said gently.

As she went over to where the sitter was standing she reflected wryly that the protective instinct in mothers was highly developed. Even as she was moving she noticed the sitter's mother mover slightly to the front, subconsciously attempting to shield her daughter. In her career, Paula had come across several instances where she had to deal with this. Unless you were trained for this, attempting to extract information from people in this frame of mind would be about as useful as attempting to get a wall to talk. *Well here goes,* she thought.

"Hello Beth" she began. Beth gave a muted sob as a reply and her mother directed a sharp glance at Paula as though willing her to stop. Paula, noting the look made up her mind. The conversation was not going to prove useful unless she got the mother out of the way.

"Ma'am" she said addressing the mother.

Another withering look.

"I think it best that I speak to Beth alone for a few minutes Mrs..?".

Beth's mother pursed up her lips. "Milton. And I gotta right to stay with my daughter through this this.." clearly she was struggling to find the words to describe the current situation. "ordeal!" she finished.

Paula sighed. *Somehow everyone you deal with has a laundry list of rights that you couldn't find anywhere the constitution. Firm but gentle handling was the key. Never let yourself get pushed around but at the same time make sure that they find your requests reasonable and not harsh.* This was what she was trained for.

She adopted a soothing tone that would have calmed an angry lioness let alone Beth's mom. "Mrs Milton I know you want to stay with your daughter but you have to realise that this is an investigation and I need to be able to have a conversation with your daughter alone without your interference. Since she was the only person at home when the child was abducted she will have to recount everything she remembers to me. I promise you that I don't intend to harass her."

Mrs Milton grudgingly obliged by moving away and saying "Don't worry Beth. You didn't do anything wrong. You tell 'em that". Morgan gave Paula a tiny nod of appreciation. *God knows we need her on the team to be able to glean any information at all* he thought. *Always get the mother away from the daughter when you deal with a teenager. Teenagers tend to lapse into lies when they are around the parents for fear of being shown up as irresponsible or reprehensible individuals.*

Paula turned back to Beth. *Oh boy! Its gonna be a long night* she thought as she met the now hostile eyes of the girl.

CHAPTER 5

A tiny glimmer of light pierced her consciousness. Then
it went away. It came back again. Caroline screwed
up her eyes. The light was getting too bright. She was jolted
awake by the memories of yesterday. She'd had a bad dream
where a man had taken her away from home. She shuddered
at the thought. Mommy would make her feel better. She had
to be near mommy now. Mommy always knew how to make
bad dreams and pains go away.

As she took in the surroundings, she felt an icy hand
grab at her chest, forcing her to stop breathing for a few
seconds. The light was coming from a dirty window near
the ceiling that was barred. A dizzying wave of shock made
her shiver as she looked at the moth eaten covers, cracked
floor boards and grimy sink at the end of the room. This
wasn't a dream. This was real. The man really had taken her
away from home. She felt tears start to prick her eyes and a
lump form inside of her throat threatening to choke her. Her
muted cry came out as a kind of stifled moan.

She froze as she saw the door at the far end of the room
open. The woman walked in with a bowl. She could see the
man lounging at the doorway, watching her through narrow

eyes as the woman made her way towards the rusty cot. She banged the tray in front of Caroline and appeared to say something. The woman suddenly spun around and looked at the man, her hands falling to her sides and shoulders straining back in fear. He appeared to be yelling at her because Caroline could see her jaw tighten as her body cringed back and her hands gripped the bars of the cot.

The woman turned back to Caroline and mimed eating. Caroline stole a glance at the man and saw him starting to walk towards the woman. Suddenly she knew without a doubt that the man was coming to hit her like he had yesterday. She turned to the woman and frantically nodded to her, signalling that she understood that she was supposed to eat what was in the bowl. The man stopped. Evidently his excuse for hitting the woman was now gone. He grimaced and abruptly turned on his heels and left. Caroline felt rather than saw the woman heave a sigh of relief. She seemed to consider something for a moment and then she too left.

Caroline was all alone in the room again.

CHAPTER 6

S arah took a deep breath as she remembered how close she had come to being beaten this morning. It was only because of the child that she had been spared. She shook herself mentally realizing that she felt grateful to the child for having understood the situation and helped her on time. *I shouldn't be getting sentimental like this. The fact that the child helped me is true but I am incapable of returning that favour in anyway.* It had happened this way a couple of times. She would start getting attached to the children. A few of them had even lasted a period of some months. She would buy them small treats from her rare visits to the store. All this was done without Alex's knowledge of course. If he got wind of her feelings, she'd be dead before the kid.

But after having lost the children she controlled her feelings and didn't get emotionally involved with any of the kids. Knowing that they were doomed and eventually going to die made the process all the more difficult. Try as she might, she couldn't stop feeling sorry for them. But there was no way she was going to get involved with this one, not if she wanted to stay sane and more importantly, alive. *I feel for you because I know your fate and that there is no escape but I can't do anything about it except pray for your soul.*

Every time a child was killed, she cried in private and prayed for the souls of the children. After years of marriage to Alex, she had stopped believing there was a God, but praying for the children had taken on the familiar form of a routine. Faith however faint, was the only thing that kept her sane.

She kept thumbing through the worn copy of the sole bible that she possessed, selecting verses that she felt were appropriate eulogies to the children who had passed on. No, been made to pass on, she thought miserably. She tried not to think about the families of the kids and the grief and fear that may be consuming them. They would never get a sense of closure, always wondering whether their children were dead, hoping they were alive and happy somewhere, but not really believing it. Or perhaps they hoped that the children were dead rather than suffer the horrible tortures that kidnappers chose to inflict on them. *Just like Alex did*, which were described in glaring detail in the news every day.

She watched dry eyed as the news on TV flashed on the faces of the children who were 'missing, presumed dead'. As she watched, she felt a thrill of fear realising that if they were caught, there would be no pardon for her. She was Alex's accomplice and the police would look at it only from that angle. *I never wanted any of this*, she silently protested to the faces on TV. I never wanted any of you to die Christina, Sylvia, Beth, Veronica..... Her mind trailed off exhausted.

Suddenly she wondered what the name of the new kid was. She probably wouldn't ever know. The way things were going, the kid would probably last a week or two. Alex had been furious that they had picked up a child who couldn't talk or hear. He had ranted about it all night. He liked to hear the kids screaming for their parents when he hit them. That wasn't going to happen with this kid. He had finally drifted off to sleep at about 3 in the morning while she lay in cold terror beside him, wondering what he was going to do to the kid on having failed him this way.

There was no point in thinking about it she told herself, as she picked up the cold untouched mug of coffee before her and went to the sink. *Don't think about the kids.*

CHAPTER 7

"So" began Paula, "can you take me through what happened?". She shifted to a more comfortable position on the hard chair on which she had to sit. She made her tone cool, impersonal though not ungentle. She noted that Beth was in extreme discomfort that had nothing to do with the seating arrangement.

Beth slowly nodded. She began hesitantly. "Go on" Paula nodded encouragingly. Beth took a deep breath. "It wasn't my fault" she started. Paula nodded. "I know that. But we have to go over the facts of the case. So tell me". This was what happened with the people who were indirectly responsible for an untoward occurrence. They always started off protesting their innocence. It always made Morgan angry when that happened. She knew what he was thinking. *What a stupid waste of time!..* She could feel anger and irritation emanating from him.

Paula motioned to him with a slight negative shake of the head. Morgan's way of dealing with people like Beth was one that many people would dearly love to follow. But that unfortunately, Paula knew, would either make her extremely hysterical or would make her stubbornly dumb, both of which needless to say would not achieve the desired result of complete cooperation.

Morgan stalked off to interview others in the neighbourhood. He figured that Paula was in her element and would probably get the girl to open up without him in the background. Paula mentally heaved a sigh of relief and suppressed a small smile. She knew what was going through his mind. It was just as well that he had left. Immediately after his departure she noticed that Beth's manner was more relaxed. She was sitting in a more comfortable way. Some people gave off an aura of anger that made everyone around them extremely aware of being near a human volcano.

She turned back to Beth. She had to suppress a mounting feeling of irritation herself. This girl was going to take forever to get to the point, she thought angrily. But it would never do to show that on her face. "I was playing with Caro in the garden" said Beth. Paula noted the emphasis on name 'Caro' in place of 'Caroline'.

I know why you used that. You want to emphasize that you and Caroline were extremely close and you would never be the cause of hurting her. Smart kid.

"Then I heard the phone ringing inside the house and I had to go in to answer it".

"Of course" Paula said. *I bet that's a lie as well darling. It's a good thing that you don't seem to know that everything you say can be verified. But I'll let you get on with it. You're doing beautifully.*

"I was inside answering the phone and Caroline was playing outside. I swear I was looking at her while answering the phone. Then I went in for a drink of water".

"And when you came out Caroline was missing" Paula didn't bother to hide the contempt in her voice. Beth looked up. For the first time she seemed to realize that Paula wasn't completely buying her story.

Paula stared right back at her. *So this is what I'll be getting from you.... For now. Once I've verified everything you've said and proved that you were not in fact taking care of the kid like you were supposed to... You'll be singing a different tune then.*

Beth was looking scared. "It's the truth detective!" her voice went up in fright.

Paula looked at her for a long moment. *I'm giving you a final chance to tell the complete truth. Don't mess it up kid.*

But it was clear that Beth was not changing her story. For the time being at least. She could see that she wasn't going to get anything more from her.

"Fine" said Paula. "We'll have other questions for you. So we will need you at the precinct for a few days. Make sure that you stay in town." For a moment, Beth thinking that she was going to be arrested, seemed on the verge of spilling her guts, but when she knew that wasn't going to happen, she composed her face onto a mask of complete innocence.

Save it for your mother kid Paula thought in disgust. She saw Beth's mom hurrying back to them, now that the interview appeared to be over. She nodded to her and went out to find Morgan.

CHAPTER 8

"Mommy mommy mommy mommy" Caroline's mind kept repeating the same words over and over again. "I feel so lost and scared mommy. I don't know what to do...". "Help me mommy, please..". Her mind felt numb. Her body felt so tired. The bed was so hard to sleep on. She didn't dare get up off the bed and move around, even in the room. The man might come and beat her like he did the woman. She missed her mommy and daddy so much, her mommy especially.

The window was almost close to the ceiling. There was no way she could get up there. She needed to go to the bathroom so badly. But there was no way she could ask the lady. They didn't understand her and she didn't know how to make them understand. She felt tears prick her eyelids again. She had cried almost the entire night and then drifted off to sleep in complete exhaustion. She had awoken as the day before because the sun was getting in her eyes.

She thought of her soft bed at home with all her stuffed toys, especially Mr. Rabbit. She'd never slept without him before. She thought of her beautiful room. But most of all she missed her mommy.

After giving her a bowl of cold oatmeal yesterday, the woman had left her alone in the room completely. She came in a few hours later to give her a bowl of cold soup and left immediately. The soup tasted real bad. But she was really hungry and so managed to gulp all of it down. Her stomach felt really queasy afterwards. But she didn't dare do anything about it.

The woman came just once more at night. She knew that because it was completely dark in the room. It was pitch dark outside where the window was. The light was switched on and the lone bulb above her bed flickered to life. A bowl of soup was pushed toward her again. The woman left the room before Caroline could do anything else.

The way the woman moved reminded Caroline of the way the man had hit her. She knew that if she didn't eat the food, the man would probably hit her again. So she drank as much of the soup as she could and poured the rest away in the sink.

When the woman had come in the room again, she'd noted with relief that the bowl was empty. She'd given a fleeting look toward the lone figure sitting hunched upon the bed and then left after switching off the light.

Now the woman entered the room again. She had another bowl with her. She set it down on the bed and grasped Caroline's arm. Caroline jumped up in fright. The woman immediately let go of her arm.

The woman shook her head in order to make her understand. She gestured out the door. She didn't seem to be able to do more than that. Caroline couldn't understand her. As she looked towards the door, she saw the man standing there like he had yesterday. He had an ugly smile on his face which made Caroline feel very scared. But she didn't dare disobey her now that the man was watching.

She stuck close to the woman's side as they made their way toward the door. As they were about to cross the threshold the man reached out as if to touch her hair. She jerked her head away in an almost reflex action. The next minute she was lying flat on the floor and seeing stars dance in front of her eyes. The man had slapped her so hard that she was disoriented for a whole two minutes before she realized what had happened. Her cheek had lost its numbness and was starting to burn with pain.

The man was standing over her, a savage look on his face. The woman stood at the far corner of the room, her face turned away from them. The man was yelling something at her. Though she couldn't hear a thing, the meaning was clear. Never under any circumstance was she to turn away from him again. The look on his face left her in no doubt of what he was capable of doing if she crossed him again.

As she lay there breathing hard and fighting tears she suddenly realized that her back felt suddenly cold. For a moment she didn't understand and then with a twist of shame she realized, that in her fear, she had wet herself. This earned her another slap as the man jumped back, a look of disgust on his face. Turning on his heel, the man left the room.

CHAPTER 9

There was nothing you could have done, Sarah told herself as she moved around the kitchen stacking the dishes in the sink. Though Alex had been in a foul mood since the morning, his sudden outburst had startled her as much as it had the child. He'd become like a bear with a sore paw just about all the time.

All she had been trying to do was get the kid to go to the john. The kid had been locked up for two nights and a day without a visit to the can. Clearly the child must have been desperate to pee. So she'd tried to take the kid to the bathroom. But she'd remembered that the kid was deaf and had to tug on the kid's arm and point toward the room. Miming was beyond her in this case and she didn't know any other way to tell the kid.

She sensed that the kid didn't understand what she was doing and didn't want to come with her. But then Alex had come to the doorway and right away she could feel the fear that he inspired in her. Somehow it angered her that Alex was powerful enough for that. Nobody had the right to do that to people and make them feel so terrified. *Damn you Alex,* she thought. She was surprised at herself for feeling this much anger against him. Fear and resentment had built up in her over the years of being married to him but the feeling of explosive anger was new to her.

The kid had acquiesced almost immediately and had come with her. Sarah had noted the way the kid kept close to her all the way to the door. She had also seen the way the kid had stiffened as they drew closer and closer to Alex. The small form shook and shivered with each step. And then Alex had to reach for her like an idiot. Anyone could see that the child was frightened to death of him. Except him, of course.

The slap he'd given her sounded like a gunshot across the room.

She'd almost thrown herself in between them but stopped herself just in time. If that had happened, she probably wouldn't be around now. Alex had a savage temper when provoked and mercilessly beat up anyone who tried to stop him doing what he wanted.

Rejection. Rejection did that to him. She'd had to learn that the hard way. It hadn't been too hard to figure out, given the number of times she'd been beaten till she lost consciousness and woken up several hours and sometimes even days later.

She'd had to turn away when he hit the child. She just couldn't watch. She had felt sorry for the other kids who'd been here but not the way she felt for this child. She tried to analyze her feelings. *Why the sudden rush of anger? Why after all these years? Was it because she wanted to protect this particular child from Alex and his insanity? But again, why? Was it because she had finally mustered up the courage to begin the fight for justice against Alex? No, that wasn't it. Maybe,* she realized, *I'm feeling sorry for the child because she already has a handicap to face in life and now is going to die just because Alex had caught sight of her.*

But she hadn't been able to stop Alex from slapping the child this morning. She could see from the corner of her eye that the child had a cut lip and was bleeding. She had been just about to move towards her when Alex slapped her again. *Why do you have to hit her now? What's she done to you, you bastard?!* She thought angrily. And then saw him, jerking his feet away. As Alex left the room, she saw the puddle on the floor and the look on the child's face. Incomprehension for a minute and then shame. Rage against Alex built up like lava in her gut.

She'd quickly walked over to the child and pulled her up, not caring for the first time that she was letting emotion register in her face. The child put up no resistance as she pulled her to her feet and half dragged her over to the bathroom. By then, some of the shock had worn off and the child was pathetically attempting to clean herself up.

She'd managed to wash and clean the child without frightening her. The child kept looking up at her as though hoping that she'd found a person who sympathised with her and would help her get out of here. The expression tore at her heart.

She'd had to quickly and a little roughly pull the child back into her room and shut the door for fear of having revealed her true feelings too much. The child already had sensed that she was more an ally than an enemy. She'd thought of what Alex would do if he had even an inkling of what was going through her mind.

The least I can do is make sure that the child does not feel completely abandoned when she dies. The thought of saving her was too ridiculous even to be entertained so this was the best she could do. *But what happens to you when she dies? How are you going to deal with that? Are you sure that you will be able to bear it? So why get emotionally involved again when you know what it can do to you? You'll be a living wreck!*, a small voice at the back of her head shouted.

At least I get to live she thought unhappily. A luxury the child will not have. I know that.

I will definitely attempt to make her more happy before the end, she vowed to herself silently. *It is the least that I can do.*

CHAPTER 10

"Negative on any kind of forced entry in the house. There is not a sign that anything is out of order. I made a thorough inspection of the grounds. A tiny vehicle, a bike precisely was found near the gate. No signs of a scuffle. If anything, the child appears to have gone of her own volition out the gate." All this was delivered in a rapid monotone in 3 seconds flat.

"Thanks Rag", Morgan nodded to him. Paula made her way over to the two of them. It was apparent that she was upset.

"Anything on the sitter?" Morgan asked.

"Nah. She's trying to be smart. She knows that we only have her word for what happened and is trying to make up a convincing story for her overlooking the fact that the kid she was supposed to watch, disappeared right in front of her eyes. But I don't think she's the perp."

"Oh. Why not?"

"She's sly but not criminal material, plus Caro's parents are not that well off. I hate to say it, but I think the girl is innocent of the crime, though her Ms Smarty Pants act is nauseating."

"Hmmm. I must say it seems bad for the kid. It's been 2 days now without a sign of her", Morgan shook his head in frustration.

"The best chance of recovery of an abducted victim is within 24 hours of the kidnapping."

"Yeah. Thanks for the heads up Raglan. That reminds me of what a fantastic job we're doing, trying to find the child." It was obvious that Paula was depressed.

"Come on Paula. Knock it off. Don't take it out on him. He is just trying to be helpful", Morgan's voice trailed off as Raglan left the room.

Paula ran a tired hand through her hair as she pulled herself up. Morgan noted with compassion that she had had no sleep at all in the last 48 hours and that somehow this case was affecting her emotionally.

"You know Paula, I used to get emotionally involved in all the cases I was part of, when I was a rookie too. I know that you know this but I suggest that you look at this from the viewpoint of a complete professional. Remember you need to keep your sanity if you want to be able to continue in this job."

"Yeah Morgan", Paula nodded in mock agreement but Morgan could see her begin to pull herself together as she left the room. Raglan came back in and sat down opposite Morgan.

"Don't be upset" began Morgan, but Raglan cut him off.

"Of course not. Individuals who are highly strung tend to be irrational and get into altercations with people around them. I understand that."

Morgan gave a small smile. Raglan, despite his social inadequacies was one of the most dependable people he had come across.

Paula came back into the room balancing three mugs of coffee in her hands. She placed the first before Morgan and went over to where Raglan sat.

"Still take hot black coffee with two sugar cubes right?".

"Yeah, that is correct", Raglan nodded.

Morgan smiled. This was Paula's way of apologising for having been short with him earlier.

The sound of a phone ringing insistently startled everyone for a minute.

Morgan picked up his phone and mouthed "Chief B" to the others.

Lieutenant Brennan was nicknamed chief B by the team because of his ability to lead the team well coupled with the knowledge of his long standing desire to become the chief of police. But this was just within their team and they didn't let it on to anyone else in the precinct.

"Yes Lieutenant, of course sir", he said into the phone. "Chief just called for a meeting", he said, pocketing his phone. "Briefing room in two minutes."

They all got up and made their way to the briefing room where the Lieutenant was already waiting for them.

"Where are we on the case?" he asked.

The good thing about the Lieutenant was that he always included himself in the team and didn't just bark out orders for the rest of the team to carry out. And when they solved a case, he gave them all their due credit without hogging all the publicity for himself.

"So, let us go over what we know so far. I think we can completely rule out the sitter as a suspect. However we will continue having her watched, just in case."

"Yes", Paula agreed. "We know that the child was abducted at approximately 17:00 hours on Monday evening. We also know that the sitter while irresponsible, did not abduct the child. Have any witnesses come forward yet? You know, it strikes me as rather extraordinary that when I have a clear cut case where I know who the perp is, I have witnesses coming out of the woodwork, trying to pinpoint someone who I know is not a criminal, but in a case like this, silence seems to be their watch word."

"That is frustrating. But we need to be able to work on our own here. We know that the child went of her own volition out of the gate, so that suggests that something piqued her curiosity enough for that to happen", Morgan was frowning intensely as though trying to see the whole picture through the eyes of a child.

"According to a quote by the US Justice Department in 1990, most strangers grab their victims on the street or try to lure them into their vehicles", Raglan piped up.

"Right. So we need to find out whether there have been any similar cases of kidnapping in the neighbouring areas. There has been no demand for a ransom of any sort, so she must have been the victim of someone who had other motives, presumably psychotic. Needless to say that this doesn't bode well for the child. We need to identify whether she is a random victim or a particular 'type', with similar age or facial characteristics of other such victims. That kind of pattern exists in most cases. Something is bound to turn up. If not, we'll have to search nationwide."

"Yes Paula, that and we have to keep an eye on the neighbours to see if they noticed even something that might help us. They may have dismissed it as irrelevant but we have to find out for ourselves."

"I personally would like to have another shot at interviewing the old lady across the street who has a good view of the garden of the girl's house. One of the other neighbours inadvertently mentioned that the old lady was in the habit of picking flowers and things from her garden in the late afternoon and evening times. If she managed to spot something, then we could really proceed faster."

Brennan had been listening with his head tilted to one side. He nodded slowly. "Yes Morgan, you may be right at that. So I want all of you to proceed doing whatever has been outlined in this discussion. I will need your reports from time to time. Please be aware that we are working against time here and may already be too late to save the child. I will have to deal with the press about this and make a statement so I need this case solved asap."

He nodded, clearly dismissing the team.

CHAPTER 11

"Why did this have to happen? And to us of all people!", Myra hadn't stopped crying since the fateful day of Caroline's abduction. Myra herself had scorned the clichéd words that came out of the mouth of every person who'd had something unfortunate happen to them. She'd always supported the theory that whatever happens to people in life depended on them alone. Now as she experienced the spine breaking sense of fear for her child, she felt the unfairness of it all.

Charles looked at her wearily and buried his face in his hands. Neither of them had slept or eaten since it happened even though neighbours and relatives had tried coaxing them to do both. He kept checking with the local police about any developments in the case but so far nothing had turned up. He too couldn't believe that something like this had happened to them. They'd had a happy life, not one of extreme wealth or glamour but one that had made them feel contented and safe. They'd been wildly happy at times and down in the dumps at others. Life had doled out its share of happiness and miseries, but they'd been able to deal with all of it and it had only strengthened them as a family.

The complications in Myra's pregnancy had almost killed her but she'd eventually managed to pull through and he was firmly convinced that it was her love for the new born child that had given her the strength to pull herself back into the world with a hitherto unknown determination.

The baby that was to have been born first had died in the womb at seven months and had plunged both Myra and him into a depression so severe that it was a miracle they ever came out of it. Only when Myra got pregnant with Caroline, did she begin to be more herself and also helped him come out of the hopelessness that he had felt the first time.

The second time around they had been so careful, following the doctor's instructions to a T by eating health foods and exercising with complete regularity. Even so the baby had refused to come out easily and had almost cost Myra her life.

But she had survived without any lasting illness. When they realised that Caroline had deaf mutism, they had been shocked and devastated. But Myra fiercely loved her daughter and strived to make her competent enough to handle the criticism to which she would surely be subject, once she came out of the comforts of a loving home into 'the real world'.

First, she had to learn to speak in a way Caroline would be able to understand and reciprocate. She'd taken lessons and practiced night and day and become proficient enough to be a teacher. One of the other things Myra thought of was to hire a baby sitter, even though she wanted to and could take care of Caroline herself. Finding a normal baby sitter was a challenge let alone one who was aware of how to use sign knowledge.

They'd finally found Beth who had a deaf younger brother and so knew how to communicate with Caroline. The biggest mistake of their lives. Charles' blood boiled whenever he thought of her. If she'd done what she was supposed to be doing, then this nightmare would never have happened. What infuriated him more was that her mother was acting as though none of this was her daughter's fault. That girl deserved to be in jail according to Charles for her cavalier disregard towards her job, for which she was being paid a large amount.

But nothing could be done about that any more.

Charles felt the hate for Beth get overshadowed by his fear for Caroline. What was happening to her now? Though he hated to acknowledge the fact, being a realist, he couldn't help but wonder whether she was alive.

Caro please please be alive, he whispered as he hugged Myra in an effort to comfort her.

CHAPTER 12

Mrs Brent woke to a miserably cold day. Her knees were killing her. The rheumatism from which she suffered got worse with every passing day and she was barely able to move on days like this.

"Good morning Peter", she whispered to the empty space beside her on the bed. This had become a morning ritual. Not a day began without her thinking about him. It was six years since he had passed on. She felt so alone without his presence. She looked around the room with unseeing eyes. The bedroom had a charming, antique Victorian appearance with pink walls, chintz chairs and a wrought iron bed. Even the bedside reading lamp was old fashioned and was more an ornament than an appliance. But none of these things registered in her brain as she gazed at them. She could still visualise Peter, standing at the sink and filling his tooth glass with water, Peter at the dinette table reading the newspaper, Peter shuffling around looking for his glasses.... Memories, memories. Everything was reduced to that.

Sighing mentally, she struggled out of the bed. Wincing at the cold, she shuffled her feet into her bedroom slippers. Tying the girdle of her housecoat more closely around her, she made her way from the bedroom to the kitchen and put on the coffee. The doctor had asked her not to drink too much coffee but to hell with him, she thought. He doesn't have to suffer the way I do. Nobody who's gone through this can grudge me a hot drink.

Reminiscing about the good old days, when she began her day by springing out of bed, fresh as a daisy, she gingerly picked up the coffee mug and went over to the dinette to have her morning coffee. Her fingers felt swollen and painful. Tears started in her eyes as she tried to hold the coffee mug more securely and ended up tipping three fourth of the coffee on the table. *Rheumatism is the devil,* she thought as she shuffled over to the kitchen and back, cleaning up the mess. With great difficulty she managed to mop up the spilt coffee and proceeded to drink the rest of it in one gulp.

She was just starting to make some toast when her bell rang. She glanced at her clock and realised that it was just past nine. People didn't make a habit of calling on her and her neighbours avoided her like the plague. *Who is it at this time of the day?* She wondered. Grumbling to herself, she walked to the door and removed the safety bolt. She could hear the person outside tapping his shoes on the porch tiles, while he waited for her to open the door. *No patience at all,* she thought with annoyance. She took her time to slowly release the catch and open the door.

It was a policeman.

Bessie Brent's first reaction was that of fear. She belonged to the old fashioned school of thought that considered members of the law enforcement bad luck. She shook herself mentally. This officer was obviously here to investigate the disappearance of the small child who lived opposite. She had known about that from her maid who did the house for her every week.

"Yes?", she asked, still not opening the door completely.

"Ma'am I need to ask you a few questions. Just a matter of routine." The officer looked at the door pointedly.

"I don't think I can help you officer." She said. But the officer looked like he had no intention of leaving.

Wincing at the pain in her knees, she opened the front door, inviting the policeman in.

CHAPTER 13

"We need to work faster Raglan", Paula said impatiently as she watched Raglan try to connect their case to other abductions.

"I need more parameters" said Raglan, who was busy feeding the relevant information that they had gathered into the system, which hopefully would turn out other similar cases in kidnapping after searching through the database. Thanks to the advancements in relational database managements and data warehousing, they were now able to rely on the system to be able to make the connections far quicker than any human mind could possibly conceive.

"Age. Similar age groups. Caroline is four". For a fleeting moment Paula fervently hoped that the usage of present tense was still valid. *Focus focus*, she told herself. "So why don't you try for children in the category of say 4 to 6 years of age."

"Mmmm hmmm..". Raglan was a computer whiz as well.

"What other things can you think of? There are too many kids in this category. We're gonna have to narrow it down big time. Like I said, every minute has approximately...."

"Ok then", Paula cut him off before he could embark on another of his little speeches. She pulled the file on the abduction off the table and rifled through the pages. What was it? She was missing something, she was sure of it. She reflected back on the picture that she had seen of Caroline at the house.

"What was it?", she shook her head in frustration. The kid had been beautiful but there were millions of children all over the place who looked angelic. She had deaf mutism. But then, the kidnapper had absolutely no way of having known that unless he'd known the family. There was the chilling possibility that the kidnapper had been keeping close tabs on the house and the occupants. That was an angle that definitely needed looking into. A person who had watched the family, had to have known that they were abducting a child incapable of speech or hearing.

Having to think like a criminal and having to place yourself in their position was mentally exhausting. But they had to go on. She had now been without sleep for 50 hours straight and that was having its toll on her.

Paula made her way over to the wash room and splashed cold water on her face, willing herself to get rid of the fatigue. A look in the mirror confirmed what she was thinking. She could see the tell tale signs from lack of rest, in the dark circles that were forming around her green eyes and the pallor of her skin reflected her exhaustion.

With honey coloured hair, deep green eyes and a jaw line many would kill for, Paula could have easily had a successful career as a model or film star. But right from when she was 12 years old, she'd been keen on becoming a detective. She'd always been different from the others in her class, preferring to watch films that reflected reality instead of the romantic comedies that the other girls seemed to love. She'd always had a fascination for detection and pored over any book that focused on crime stopping. Growing up, her favourite books had included Sherlock Homes and the Poirot mysteries. So it was rather predictable that she'd end up as a cop, though her parents wanted her to pursue something else.

As she walked over to the coffee machine, she mulled over the facts of the case. She wondered where Caroline was and whether she was alive at that very moment.

"It may be too late to save her but I swear I'll find out who did this", she vowed to herself, as she picked up the coffee mug and headed back to Raglan.

CHAPTER 14

"Well ma'am", began Morgan. He sat opposite the old woman, in her living room.

The living room was surprisingly comfortable with soft, well worn couches, a carpet in tones of red and deep green, a tall leather armchair on which he was ensconced comfortably, wide windows that faced the lawn and an antique chandelier that was a beautiful piece of work.

"Before you begin officer, I have to tell you that I know you must be here to ask me about the abduction that happened a couple of days back from across the street. I am absolutely sure that I have nothing important to tell you."

Wow, thought Morgan, *and I haven't even started yet. This lady is one tough cookie and has decided to resist all my attempts to coax information out of her.* He suddenly wished Paula were here as she was the one who was best suited to this kind of job. But the idea to interview this lady had been his, so Brennan wanted him to get on with it. *Here we go,* he thought.

"I am sure that you would have told me if there had been anything important that you knew, ma'am". He made his voice sound earnest and sincere. "This is just a mere matter of routine, something that we have to do", he said, and was rewarded by the slight softening of the old woman's face.

"Do you think you can cast your mind back to what happened two days ago? Just a sketch of all that went on that day". He'd been about to mention that the chatty neighbour had confided about the gardening habits of Mrs. Brent and the likeliness of her having seen what happened, for his nature was to get to the point immediately without beating around the bush. But he stopped himself at the last minute, somehow sensing that he wouldn't get anywhere if he rushed with this old bird. So he strived to make his voice sound softer and more relaxed. He was finding it difficult, but he had to go on.

"Hmmm, if you insist", Mrs. Brent said in a maddeningly weary voice. Morgan felt his jaw tighten in anger, *a child has been abducted and you sit here acting as though the weight of the world is on your shoulders when I ask you a question that may save her life and help apprehend the monster who abducted her.* A minute later he felt ashamed of himself, when he saw her wincing with pain she moved her knees and the way her fingers were almost deformed with acute arthritis. Being in excellent health himself, made him appreciate that others, especially old people did not have that luxury. She probably was in the beginning stages of Alzheimer's too, at her age. No wonder she found it tough to have to remember today's breakfast let alone what she did a couple of days back. He must learn to be more patient, a gift that came naturally to people like Paula. So he smiled encouragingly at her, prompting her to answer.

"Let's see, I woke up at my usual time which is around seven and made coffee". She frowned in an effort to remember.

"Once that was done, I made, what was it?, scrambled eggs I think. It was really tough to crack the eggs open without spilling the yolk..." she stopped self consciously, seemingly aware that she was telling things that would certainly never be entered on record in a police file.

But the officer didn't seem impatient at all. He was just listening to her politely which was surprising considering he couldn't wait two minutes for her to open the door. In six years, no one had listened to anything Bessie Brent had to say including her maid, who did what she liked despite instructions. So like a dam bursting she began to pour out every trivia that she remembered, on what had happened on the day of Caroline Winters' abduction.

CHAPTER 15

Myra opened her eyes slowly. She hadn't slept at all for the past few days and sometime last night she had dozed off into a fitful sleep which was punctuated with painful dreams. She had never been able to remember her dreams before this but today the vivid recollection of her dreams startled her. All of them had involved her watching helplessly as she watched Caroline being devoured by a weird black mist.

The last one had been particularly scary as it was almost realistic in its vividness. She and Caroline had been walking on the beach and Charles had gone to get ice cream after making sure what flavours they wanted. She was holding Caroline by the hand and slowly strolling down the beach, letting the soft breeze ruffle her hair and the waves curl around her toes, a welcome coolness pervading her feet as the sun blazed overhead. The silence was peaceful making her feel rested. As she looked around lazily, she slowly became aware that her hand was clutching empty air and she couldn't feel the presence of Caroline nearby. Coming out of her reverie in a shock, she looked around frenziedly for any sign of Caroline. She saw in the far distance, a bulky figure with a dark hooded jacket with something thrown over his shoulder. As she squinted her eyes to get a better look, she realized with disbelief that the something was in fact Caroline. She began to run after him, yelling for him to stop. But he continued to move as though he hadn't heard anything. The frightening thing was that he never changed pace and continued onward in the same heavy tread. She was running as fast as her feet could take her, yet never seemed to be getting any nearer to him. He was moving farther and farther away. He slowly turned and looked at her once before disappearing into the horizon.

It was after this that she woke up with a feeling of absolute dread in the pit of her stomach. She felt the familiar tears course through her cheeks as she realized that Caroline was still missing. The police were trying to be optimistic but she was not an idiot. She'd read once somewhere that it was very difficult to trace a child after it had been missing for a day.

Charles also tried to have a more positive outlook but she knew that he was doing that for her. He was also possibly going mad with worry over what may have happened to Caro. She loved her daddy and she was his pet. Both of them had done virtually nothing these few days and just sat around looking like zombies, hoping against hope that a miracle would grant them their child back.

A look in the bathroom mirror confirmed what she thought. She looked lifeless. She felt as though something inside her had died. Her eyes moved onto Charles who had also fallen asleep after trying to reassure her that they were doing everything they could to get Caroline back. By 'they' he meant the police. But she knew he was as worried as her that they hadn't been able to make much headway so far.

Myra thought back to the time when they first realized she was pregnant for the second time. She'd just started her job as a professional sculptor in a small art agency and Charles had already been working in a firm as an accountant.

They were so happy when they realized that she was 'in the family way', the second time around. After the first trauma, they had been so careful the second time. They'd looked around for a suitable place to live for six long months. And then they'd found it. A tiny two bedroom apartment which was charming and which they'd thought would be perfect for their child. The apartment owner, who had also had similar humble beginnings had been willing to rent it for a low price. They'd moved in, full of hopes and dreams for a great future.

She remembered what fun they'd had shopping for baby clothes in small thrift shops and stores, looking around, hunting through stuff and finding surprisingly good clothes at rates that were dirt cheap. They didn't have enough money to furnish the apartment properly, but we both tried to make it comfortable and cheerful with whatever little we had, like plants on the windowsills and a hand hooked rug that she made, in the living room. We painted the house ourselves, she remembered, using cheerful vibrant colours.

Going through the thrilling ambiguous feeling of whether it was going to be a boy or a girl, for the second time and the joy of realizing that finally we had a beautiful daughter of our very own. The shock when we realized that the baby had a terrible problem called deaf mutism. They'd never dreamed they'd have any problem like that.

She also remembered how hard they'd fought against the idea and the finally accepted it. The fierce need to learn sign language and the struggle to make Caro feel that nothing was wrong with her, make her feel loved despite her trouble.

They'd moved to this new place just a year back. Charles had gotten a job in a bigger firm and her talent for sculpting was just beginning to be recognized and appreciated. She had just got her first big break eight months previously when a big art firm had hired her for their new project.

They'd been ecstatic about the move over to a larger more spacious place and she loved Minneapolis for its cold weather. They had been thinking about getting Caroline a dog because she had been asking for one. It could keep her company if they had to go out without her.

Maybe if we'd done that sooner Caro would still be here, she thought. *Oh Caro Caro!! Where are you??*

She went downstairs and dug out her ivory rosary beads, a present from her grandmother when she was fifteen. Granny had always been religious and she had also had to attend mass every Sunday growing up. But as she grew older, she'd gone through the usual stages of boredom, fatigue and atheism and finally stopped going to Church altogether.

She never had dreamed that she would begin praying again until now. Keeping her eyes closed and fingering her rosary beads she began to pray quietly.

Lord, please spare me my child. Please let nothing happen to Caroline. Please bring her back to me safe and sound....

CHAPTER 16

Why on earth is my brain moving so sluggishly? I know that I'm missing something. Paula kept moving her head in frustration. *Damn!* Paula knew that there was something lurking in the recesses of her mind, elusive, evading capture, refusing to come to the forefront of her mind. What had triggered that memory?

She had an idea that it had something to do with her memory of Caroline's face. Ever since she'd seen that picture she'd been haunted by something. The feeling of awareness that something, some kind of familiarity, was growing stronger with every passing minute. It hadn't been such a persistent knowledge at first. But now she was sure that there was some kind of pattern she was seeing here. She could feel that if she managed to pin what it was, they would be so much closer to knowing who the kidnapper was.

Morgan strode into the room. He gave a quick glance at Paula and was shocked by what he saw. She was the closest thing to a zombie he had ever seen. Her face was white, her pupils enormous and she sat without moving, as though she were in a trance of some sort.

"Paula", he called as he went over to her. Paula was too deep in thought. She didn't move. "Paula!" Morgan's voice was sharper, but still didn't evoke a response. "Paula!!" he shouted and he shook her. She came out of her reverie with a jerk and gazed in disorientation at her surroundings.

"What the hell is wrong with you?!" Morgan yelled. "You've got to pull yourself together! What is happening? You look sick!"

"Nothing nothing is wrong. I'm fine", Paula mumbled, embarrassed to have him reprimand her twice in a day.

"I'm going to request Brennan that he pull you out of this case. This is getting almost personal. You seem to be too emotionally attached to this victim. You are not able to think objectively. Go home and get some shut eye. You look worn out", Morgan's voice was getting progressively softer as he eyed her.

"No, no! Please don't do that!", Paula's voice rose to a shriek as she realised the implications what he was saying. "I really am fine Morgan. Please believe me!", she tried to compose herself so as to make him trust her.

"Absolutely not Paula! I prefer to trust my own eyes. And it's obvious that you are too close to this case, given that you look like hell."

"No really Morgan", Paula's voice took on a steely note as she eyed him. "I give you my word I am fine. I am not close to the victim at all. Do I empathise with her? Absolutely. Because I've seen what can happen to victims of an abduction, especially young children. As it turns out, it is a job requirement that I know how to deal with the victim's families and I have found that the best way to do that it to actually identify with their emotions without faking an understanding, because what you actually feel will come through in the end."

Morgan had listened to everything she said, a frown between his brows. "I agree that you will have to empathise with them but this is too much Paula. There is a fine line between being able to appreciate a person's feelings and actually feeling it yourself. That's what you've been doing here, instead of being the shrink, you've become the patient!"

"Not really Morgan. Since you seem so insistent, I'm going to tell you, something has been preying on my mind, these past few days. I've seen something just like this before. There is some kind of pattern that can be established. I am just not seeing it now."

Morgan looked closely at her and realised that she was telling the truth. That meant that her input, provided she got it on time could make or break the case. Cognizant of the consequence of knowledge she was trying to remember he said, "Fine. I'll not talk anymore about you quitting this case kiddo, but you're going to have to figure out a way to get this information without killing yourself in the process. By the way even I've managed to uncover some important information from the old lady who lives across the girl's house. Meeting in the briefing room in fifteen. Bring Raglan along. I'll inform the chief. I want everyone to hear this. Meanwhile keep sifting through your mind and try to find out what the connection is."

Paula gave a wan smile. "Aye aye Captain", she said as she resolutely turned back to the file of the case on her desk.

CHAPTER 17

Sarah moved around the bedroom quietly so as not to wake Alex up. He'd drunk himself into a coma last night and it would be a long time before he woke up, she hoped. As she slipped out of the room quietly, she reflected on what happened yesterday. Alex had come home only in the evening after he had left so abruptly in the morning. After cleaning up Caroline and taking her back to her room, she'd immediately heated a cup of milk and proceeded to make a cup of hot chocolate. Vague memories of her father making hot chocolate for her when she got home from school and how she'd felt warm and happy almost immediately afterwards, made her think of doing the same for the child.

When she went into the room, she found Caroline huddled up in the corner of her cot shivering. She saw Caroline's eyes fill up with tears as she handed her the cup and she wondered what had brought on the tears. Maybe she never expected a kindness from her or maybe the gesture had triggered a happy memory like it had for her. She felt her own eyes beginning to fill up at the child's expression and had had to turn away. The child had looked so vulnerable.

She was vulnerable. There was nothing she could do to stand up against a brute like Alex.

The rest of the day until the evening had proceeded in comparative peace and quiet. She'd made the child a peanut butter and jelly sandwich for lunch, again remembering that she'd loved it as a child. The child ate every bite of it, she was evidently very hungry. In an attempt to calm her down, she'd put her arms around the child, hugging her.

For a moment she felt the child stiffen in fear, the trembling little body held taut and hard against her. Then seeming to realise that she wasn't going to be hurt, she'd relaxed against her and hugged her tightly in turn. The child began sobbing unrestrainedly, her body shaking with emotion, the fear that she had felt, the longing to get back home, the loneliness without her mother. In that one moment, Sarah understood who a mother was and what she meant in a child's life.

She'd gently rocked the child back and forth, making hushing little noises of comfort forgetting for the moment that she couldn't hear. It was quite a long time before she slept, the sobs growing quieter and the harsh breathing easing slowly to a quiet pattern. At some point she herself had dozed off without changing her position.

It was the sound of the car pulling into the driveway that woke her. She woke up with a jerk almost dislodging the child. But the child was evidently too exhausted and did not wake. A glance at her watch told her it was almost six pm. She'd left the room quickly and gone into the den and hastily switched on the TV, pretending to watch it just as Alex entered.

Alex was unusually quiet. He'd gone straight to the bedroom and stayed inside for the next couple of hours, not venturing outside even for a glass of water. She'd wondered about it as she got dinner ready. It wasn't like him to be so taciturn. Lord knew she preferred it to his usual abuse but it was starting to bother her a lot. She managed to slip into the child's room and feed her before he made an appearance.

He'd come out at about half past eight and eaten his dinner in front of the TV, choosing to remain quiet through the entire meal. Once dinner was over and she was stacking the dishes in the sink she saw him pacing restlessly in the den, frequently glancing at the clock and scowling. He made as if to go to the bedroom, apparently changed his mind and came into the kitchen. This again was an unusual thing to do. He had hardly ever set foot inside the kitchen since they came to this house, considering it to be her domain. Alex didn't usually enter places where he didn't feel like the boss.

She'd glanced up at him and astonishment but had wisely chosen to keep her mouth shut. Even the Alex she normally saw was an unpredictable man at the best of times. She wasn't fool enough to start something that might end in her getting unconscious or worse.

Alex clearly had been uncomfortable. He kept fidgeting and tapping his feet against the tiles, picking up random things from the counter and shoving them back haphazardly. Still he didn't say anything. He seemed to be at a loss for words. She'd prayed that her silence shouldn't act as an irritant to him and provoke him to beat her up.

Finally he seemed to come to some internal decision. "Sarah", he'd said, "We need to leave here by tomorrow evening, so get everything packed."

She hadn't known what to say and had just gazed at him in astonishment for a few minutes and then nodded silently, before turning back to the sink.

He'd seemed to feel that an explanation was needed even though she hadn't said anything. "I've got an offer I can't refuse. I'd be a fool to let it go."

Again she'd glanced up at him trying to hide her surprise. Since when had Alex cared about anything like a good job offer? He made enough as a mechanic in a repair shop that was about twenty five minutes from the house. Until now he'd never looked for a better job or anything like that.

He'd seemed to know what was going through her mind. He'd gazed at her in apparent amusement at her naiveté. And smiled. It had been a cruel smile, a gloating smile, but there had been something else in it too, something that was hard to define. *So the discomfiture was a pretence. Or had his curiosity got the better of him and he intended to find out something?* His next words had chilled her to the bone.

"I was talking to Joe over at the bar and he said that he knew of someone, someone rich who will be willing to pay me a hell of a lot, enough to make me rich for a lifetime", he'd paused deliberately "for the girl."

She remembered hoping fervently that the shock she felt wasn't shown on her face. But she'd seen him toying with the idea of letting her in on the plan. He'd deliberately chosen to tell her. *Why?* It was not his normal practice. He simply told her what to do and she did it, no questions asked. And he had never sold any of the other kids. He took them only to gratify his sadistic whims. He had too much fun maiming them and hearing them scream and yell for their parents, relishing their powerlessness, finally killing them when they could no longer scream. He'd never thought of the money angle until now.

Why then had he told her what he was going to do? He'd definitely been watching her for her expression. So... He knew. Knew that she loved the child and wanted to protect her. Or was it a shot in the dark to see if the news upset her. Dear God I may have just given myself away, she remembered thinking. But how on earth had he found out? She'd been so careful, never showing anything that would lead him to suspect what she was thinking.

But she'd once read somewhere that some people had a kind of sixth sense and could make out whether emotions were real or faked. It could also mean that she was simply a bad actress. Either way there was no going back now.

She'd made up her mind to rescue the child. She had a fair idea of what the 'rich guy' would do to the child once she was his. She wouldn't be able to help her then. She'd lain tossing all night wondering what she could do. Alex had proceeded to get himself intoxicated to the point of losing consciousness. Probably in an obscure part of his mind, he was already regretting the decision, for having lost the pleasure of bringing about a violent end to the child's life himself, if not for anything else. But Alex was smart and some part of his brain also suspected her. So he also could have pretended to become drunk. He'd definitely been drunk enough times in reality to be capable of playing the part to perfection. She had to act quickly. The snores coming from the bed seemed to be real. Alex also had the disadvantage of believing that she had no gumption. She'd never been bold enough to do anything about his actions before, no matter how cruel they'd been. So he may have just wanted to torment her by increasing her feeling of helplessness. All these thoughts had gone through her mind as she lay awake. They had made her more afraid. But surprisingly she had also never felt more brave as she realised she was going to at least attempt to save the girl. For the first time she appreciated that life was bigger than just her. This decision had taken a long time to make and she was going to stand by it no matter what came.

CHAPTER 18

Paula, Raglan and Brennan looked at Morgan as he began telling them what he'd learnt. They were all assembled in the briefing room and since Morgan had called the meeting, Brennan had simply started off by saying "Officer Morgan has something important to report. Over to you, Morgan" and moved over so that Morgan could address them all.

Morgan began by telling them that he'd followed up on his idea of interviewing the old lady opposite.

"She was a bit uncooperative at first but then proceeded to tell me that she had been in the garden, just like the neighbour said. She usually goes out into the garden at about 3 in the afternoon and by some freak chance, she'd had to do something that day, like clean out the kitchen cabinets or whatever and so could go out only at about four thirty. She admits that she didn't particularly look around and was concentrating on picking flowers. However she did see a car, a station wagon of a deep brown colour, which was unfamiliar cross their street. She didn't think much of it and went back into the house. From the window of the house she saw a couple get out. The man opened up the hood and did something."

"You'd think she should have come forward with this sooner.." began Brennan, when Morgan said "Oh and she noticed Caroline cycling in the garden. It was easy to notice her because of her bright red hair, she said."

Paula suddenly let out a long sigh of comprehension. "Of course" she said. "The hair".

"Yes Paula", Morgan sensed that they were getting to the truth at last. The net was closing, he could feel it. "You've realised what the connection is?"

"Yes and at the risk of sounding clichéd, I was a fool not to have seen it earlier. The hair, that's what's been bothering me all along. I knew I'd seen a similar case, I just never thought that the hair was the similarity. About a year before I started working here I came across a case of two children being abducted who were about the same age as Caroline, also. There was absolutely no connection between the families and believe me we checked everything from parish records to dental records. Nothing to tie them together, except that both the children had red hair. I should have remembered it! We didn't manage to solve that one and the children are still listed in the police files as 'missing presumed dead'".

"If you could tell me the details of where this children used to live, I could try to find out more about the abduction."

"Get to it at once", ordered Brennan. "I've a gut feeling we're going to nab these bastards and when we do..." his voice trailed off but the expression on his face left no one in any doubt of what he would do.

CHAPTER 19

As Sarah made her way downstairs, she thought she heard the bed creak and she stopped still, her heart pounding. If Alex caught her, she would have to simply act normal, like she'd gone downstairs to make the coffee. As the seconds passed agonizingly, she gripped the banister and prayed that he was still asleep. Fate seemed to favour her as no more sounds were heard and the house remained silent.

She went down the steps soundlessly and walked over to the room where the child was kept. Quietly she went over to the bed where the child lay sleeping. Any doubts about what she was doing, the risk she was putting herself in, vanished when she looked at the sleeping face of the child. In the past few days she wondered why she hadn't helped the other children. Maybe if she had done this before, Alex would be in prison by now and all the other kids he'd murdered would have been safe and have grown up to have normal happy lives.

How many times would she have repeated the line *Bless me father for I have sinned?* She'd lost count of the number of times she'd said that. She suddenly realized that she had stood here, in this very spot, watching Alex beat those other children to death, unable to do anything to stop him and praying for those children. Her Bible was the only thing that had kept her sane all those years.

And now.... Now she was going to make sure the child reached her parents safe. *How long had she been standing here reminiscing?* Alex could wake up anytime now. She had to move fast.

She bent over the child and gently shook her awake. The child woke up at once and looked around, frightened and confused. A few days here and she'd become a light sleeper, waking at the slightest touch, Sarah thought.

She motioned to the child to come with her. The child looked as though she might refuse, but something in her face seemed to touch the child and she came willingly with her. They moved silently out the room and opened the front door quietly.

As Sarah looked around, she saw the car standing in the driveway, where Alex had parked it last night. In his hurry to tell her the news, he'd forgotten the keys and they still hung there in the ignition. She started towards the car but stopped suddenly. It was as though someone had thrown a dash of cold water against her face. *What if Alex had deliberately left the keys in the car? It was as though he were enticing her into a trap. He was normally very meticulous which was why he'd never been caught all these years. It wasn't like him to leave his car keys hanging in the ignition, no matter what the hurry.* She stood there for a moment, undecided.

She felt the child, shiver beside her. It was pretty early and no one in the neighbourhood was up yet. It was still dark, though she could see the light slowly beginning to penetrate the darkness. She lifted up the child and bundled her into her coat, tucking the child's legs around her and pressing her close to her own body in an attempt to keep her warm. The child snuggled up to her, her soft breathing coming out like smoke in the cold.

In that moment, the greatest temptation in her life came to Sarah. What if she could take the child away and go away somewhere, away from Alex, away from the life she'd known all these years and go someplace new with the child and start afresh. She really loved the child and in time the child would learn to love her as well. But as she looked down at the tiny form in her hands, she pictured her losing the child to someone and living on. She knew then that she couldn't do it to someone, no matter how much the child meant to her.

She moved quickly, lest she change her mind about leaving the child with her parents. Up the driveway and out the front gate in a minute and then she proceeded up the road. She considered hiring a taxi for herself but Alex would be bound to find out since he knew all the guys who worked there. She had no illusions about her life once she'd returned the child, some part of her was sure Alex would find her and kill her. But if she escaped, she was going away from here, to someplace warm, she just hated the cold, maybe someplace with a beach. She had some money that she'd scrimped and saved which would tide her over until such time that she could find a job.

She moved purposefully up the road in a fast stride, uttering a small prayer she'd made up.

Dear God, please spare me and this child, please let us get away safely and let the child be returned to her parents safe. Grant me my life please please please....

CHAPTER 20

Sarah began to sweat slightly as she hoisted up the child slightly and walked faster. The child was starting to feel like a lead weight and she was afraid that if she put her down and asked her to walk along, it would impede the speed of progress. She had to get away as far as possible from Alex. There still was so much distance to cover. There was no tram in sight and as luck would have it, no cab either. The only cab that had passed had not even slowed when she tried to flag it down. Resigned, she had begun walking for what felt like an hour or two but was in fact just twenty minutes. The little beads of perspiration on her forehead froze when the cold morning air brushed against her.

She began to pant slightly and the rapid movement made the child wake up and look around blearily. Shock then fear registered on her face as she saw that they were on the road. She tried to squirm but Sarah held her firmly and shook her head, looking straight ahead. After a few minutes of squirming the child appeared to accept the fact that it wasn't going to be put down and settled for quietly watching both her and the road alternately.

She had to walk another forty blocks or so to reach the neighbourhood of the child and that thought made her exhausted. She had started out of the house with only the money that she'd saved and nothing else because she had been afraid of delaying the escape further and have Alex wake up and come after her. Now as she panted, out of breath, she realized that her mouth was parched and she needed something to drink very badly. The thought that Alex might catch up with them anytime made her walk faster but after a few yards, she realized that she wasn't going to be able to move further without some kind of sustenance.

She spied a store that was just being opened up by a guy, presumably the owner and thankfully made her way over to it.

"Early bird eh?" he said as she walked in right behind him.

She gave him a non committal nod and made her way over to the aisles and began picking up snacks and juice.

The man realizing that she was going to be non communicative, went behind the billing counter and began to boot his computer.

As she picked up everything she would need and made her way over, she heard a slight noise to her left. Someone had come in at the door.

She reflexively turned her head and met the eyes of her husband.

CHAPTER 21

"Got anything yet", Paula asked Raglan as they both watched the computer, with Raglan quickly feeding the new inputs he'd they'd obtained. While the assumption of the victims' age group alone, did not help them narrow down the list, the addition of the physical characteristic that Paula had identified as being common to two of the previous known victims brought the number considerably down.

"It looks like about twenty five children in that age group with red hair have been reported as missing in the past seven years. The locations where the children have been lost are not always from homes. They have been apparently lost in shopping malls, theatres, the general places you except families with children to go and once even at a funeral" Raglan finished disbelievingly.

"Looks like the couple have made a complete job of it. I don't understand why the connection has never been made before, so many children, all with red hair and no one noticed??", Morgan sounded both incredulous and incensed.

"Yeah well until you gave me that little bit of information, which was in fact given to you by an old woman past seventy with much diminished facilities, I didn't make the connection either", Paula seemed disgusted with herself.

Morgan said nothing.

"I think the reason for the late discovery of the pattern has trivial connection to anyone's sensory capabilities", said Raglan, as usual taking the comment literally. "The victims have been chosen at random areas, so this was apparently not planned. That worked in the abductors' favour. Even we were able to spot the connection only because we were looking for it in particular. The geographical domain is quite large. We are looking for someone who lives in Minneapolis because the children have been abducted all through the year. No specific job type presents itself as there are no indicators of the abductions happening in specific times of the year. So my guess would be that the job would be one where he has a lot of opportunity to be mobile through the day and through the year."

Paula nodded. "Fine. Go ahead and work your magic with that information and find us some answers fast."

Raglan turned back to the computer, this time mercifully with no repartee about there being no magic involved in the algorithm and only logic giving the answers.

They were interrupted by a call from a man who was apparently outside a store and could see a guy holding a gun to a woman. The caller was a talker and was describing in detail what the man looked like from the back and the woman's appearance as well. "Oh and there is a child of about four or five as well", he added "with bright red hair".

For a split second Morgan looked at Raglan and Paula, their faces reflecting what he himself was thinking.

"Yeah yeah. We got it" Paula motioned to Morgan. "Inform Chief B and let's get the hell out of here!"

Morgan pulled out his cell phone as they made their way out. "Lieutenant Brennan, we think we found our man. We need to get there to check it out. There is apparently a station wagon of said description parked outside the place. I have a hunch that this is the abductor. A child who looks like Caroline is said to be inside at gun point. We need to be there at once Chief B."

"Good work. Get on it right away and also take a few people with you. The perps are armed and I don't want the situation getting out of hand now. I'll be there shortly, just tell me the place. Use your siren. It might be the only way of saving the child now, letting them know they've been nabbed. Make it quick. I want a clean job of it. The child, if she is alive will be our priority and try to bring in the abductors alive but not at the cost of the child."

"Right away sir". Morgan cut off the call and stowed his phone back in his pocket. "We need to take along a couple of others."

"Chief's orders", he added as he saw Paula opening her mouth to protest.

She nodded once and they went out of the station with Morgan flagging a couple of guys in the precinct and asking them to come along with the team.

It was almost like déjà vu as Raglan started the car, with Paula sitting at the side and Morgan behind. Only Brennan was missing. The other guys followed close behind as the cars raced forward to where they hoped Caroline would be.

CHAPTER 21

S arah gasped.
    She felt like she'd been punched in the gut, winded.
All her hope was crushed in one instant.

It was almost an involuntary action that her eyes went over to where he had his right hand hidden inside his jacket. She could see a bulge, a faint outline of....

"Going somewhere sweetheart?" Alex's voice was mild, pleasant even. He couldn't have been more casual if he'd been enquiring about the weather. His face showed absolutely no emotion except perhaps what could be construed as a mild interest in her travel plans.

The child had turned at the same time as she had and now her face registered utter terror.

Sarah's mind was running around like a squirrel in a cage. *How? How? How?* Her mind kept asking repeatedly. Instinctively she took in her surroundings. There was absolutely no other customer in the store and it looked like it was going to stay that way for some time. There was no way she was getting help from that quarter. A slight repositioning of her eyes showed her that the guy at the billing counter was eyeing them with slight interest. He seemed to realize that they were talking, but he apparently put it down to friendly chitchat and made no move except to plug on the earphones of his ipod and turn towards his system, in relaxed contemplation.

Alex saw her checking.

"What are you looking for, honey? You look real scared. You're not afraid of me, are you? I just came to help you pick out the groceries..." As his eyes roamed over her shopping cart, his lips curved in an ingratiating smile which quickly turned to a sneer.

"Why did you have to bring the kid along? She could have slept back home while you and I shopped couldn't she? What kind of a mother are you, dragging a small child around in the wee hours of the morning to shop? She must be feeling pretty drowsy.... I am going to see to it that she gets put to sleep", he paused "properly from now..."

His meaning couldn't have been clearer.

"Give. The. Kid. To. Me", Alex precisely enunciated every syllable slowly, his eyes locked on hers, his hands moving closer.

The child squirmed in fear and moved closer to her, burying her face inside Sarah's sweater.

"What were you thinking, darling? Did you really think you could get away from me that easily. I love you too much to give up like that", he snapped his fingers and leered at her. "Were you going to save the little darling?" he said, looking at the child. "My God! I really have to give it you sugar! You've a lot of courage to try to help her.... Or were you going to screw her over for some deal of your own?", he frowned momentarily as though he himself was surprised at what he'd said. Sarah could see that he was musing to himself. "Could be, could be.... I'd never have pegged you for a spunky broad but what you've done today shows me I've been very wrong, doesn't it ..."

"Doesn't it?" he added more slowly.

Sarah still wasn't able to say anything.

Alex moved closer.

The guy at the counter wasn't even looking at them.

"Well, well, well looks like I am going to have to pick her up myself after all..."

And then the child screamed. Scream after scream rent the air in continuous succession.

Alex jumped back in reflex, jarred for an instant by the unexpected sound.

The scream had the effect of snapping Sarah out of her inability to move. She tried to run, pushing the cart towards Alex in a feeble attempt to deter his onslaught.

The guy at the counter heard the screams over the sound of his music and snapped around in time to see Alex pull out his revolver and fire it, missing her and the kid, but getting a bag of chips instead which promptly exploded sending a shower of crisps to the floor.

"Hey!!! What in hell do you think......", he never finished his sentence as a bullet exploded into his head, spewing blood and bits of brain on the wall and he promptly slumped against his chair.

Sarah was petrified at the sight of the dead guy at the counter. No pity for him registered as she began running zigzagged down the aisle with the child. Only fear for herself.

As the distant sounds of a police siren rent the air, she felt a bullet whistle past her right ear and embed itself in the wall opposite her. The next shot hit her neck and she fell forward, cradling the child with her arms trying not to crush her.

As she felt her eyes begin to close she saw a dozen images shooting through her mind. Scenes from her childhood, flashes of her life, faces of the children Alex murdered. Her final image was her mom imploring her not to marry Alex because she was afraid of the man he was, the man he could be. *You were right mom. How right....* was her last thought as she sighed and her body shuddered and went still.

CHAPTER 22

Paula was the first one out of the squad car, as it squealed to a stop outside the store. Morgan and Raglan were on her heels as the ran towards the store.

"Paula and Joe! Back entrance! Now!" Morgan yelled over the sound of gunshots that could be heard in rapid succession inside the store. Paula nodded and ran towards the back of the store with Joe. The sound of another police siren indicated the arrival of Brennan.

Morgan, Raglan and Sam moved to the front entrance of the store with their guns levelled. There was dead silence inside.

Morgan could see a guy behind the counter dead. *Jesus Christ* he thought as he saw the hole in his head and bits of brain splattered against the wall.

He motioned with his eyes to Raglan and Sam to move to the sides, looking down each aisle. It wasn't a very big store and they would be able to sweep the entire area for the child quickly. Morgan felt a tap on his shoulder and saw Brennan behind him, also with his gun levelled. An inspection of the next aisle revealed the body of a woman, who matched the description given by the caller as the one holding the child. But the child was not near her.

Before they could go any further, they saw a man step out from behind a cluster of shopping carts, half dragging Caroline and pointing a revolver to her head.

"Let us go or I swear I will shoot her."

The guy's voice had none of the strain that Morgan had seen with a lot of thugs who took hostages. There was no hurry, no fear. He was simply observing a statement of fact. The guy looked to be in his late thirties with a calm face and demeanour.

Morgan could see that there would be no reasoning with this guy, no matter how experienced a professional. There were some people who could be coaxed or be made to put down their weapons by firm talking. That wouldn't work here.

Nevertheless it was necessary to at least try if they had a hope of getting the child out of this alive.

"Put your weapon down and listen to me."

Brennan was making an attempt to get through to him.

"Or what?". The man sneered at them. He tightened his hold on the revolver and pushed it harder against Caroline's face.

"There is no way out of this for you. It would be in your best interest to let the child go and come quietly. We will be forced to shoot you down otherwise."

Sometimes offensive speech worked when the perpetrator was jolted into reality that there was no escape whatsoever. Not this time.

"You think I don't know that dodo? And what? You gonna shoot me down at the price of getting her killed?"

he grinned. He deliberately kicked Caroline hard, while intentionally maintaining eye contact with Brennan. The child cried in pain.

Morgan gritted his teeth in anger. He felt Brennan tighten his jaw in frustration and anger. Out of the corner of his eye, he espied Paula and Joe move silently from behind the man. Brennan noticed them as well and nodded almost imperceptibly.

The man had apparently not heard them come up from behind him because he was completely focussed on Brennan. But he did notice the slight nod that Brennan gave and whirled around.

But he was too late. Paula's shot hit him straight at the temple and he crashed down lifeless on top of Caroline.

Paula immediately caught hold of his body and tugged him off of the child who was screaming in fear. As she hugged the child and instinctively rocked her back and forth making soft soothing noises, forgetting for the moment that the child could not hear, Morgan walked over to her.

"You're safe now. You're ok", Paula was saying over and over again.

Morgan smiled. "Thanks to you, she *is* safe *now*."

CHAPTER 23

M yra was praying when the telephone rang. For a moment she was tempted to not answer it thinking of the number of people who'd called in the past two days to offer their condolences. Almost like they believed Caroline was dead. She didn't want to listen to the pity in their voices, telling her how sorry they were that such a terrible thing had happened. Right now all she wanted was hope. But some instinct told her to answer the phone.

She had been praying continuously for the past eight hours. Rosary in hand, she kept repeating her prayer over and over, requesting God to help her and not abandon her, keep Caroline safe wherever she was and more importantly to return her to them.

Reluctant yet hopeful, she answered the call. The voice at the other end told her that Caroline had been rescued from her abductors and was taken to the police station in Nicollet Avenue. She was being brought home right now and would reach there in a few minutes.

"Charles! Charles!", Myra was screaming as she put down the receiver, tears of joy running down her face.

As Charles came running down in a panic, she said between sobs "They've found her. They're bringing her over now. Right now..."

"God! Thank God! Thank you! Thank you!!!" Charles was crying as he came towards her, eyes alight with relief and happiness. Then Myra did the most natural thing in the world, under the circumstances. She fainted.

CHAPTER 24

"And so finally, we were able to bring her back to you", Paula finished as she got up ready to go.

Myra and Charles had been listening with both their arms around Caroline who had fallen asleep between them on the couch. They couldn't touch her enough, the miracle they'd come so close to losing forever.

When she had been brought home, they'd rushed both her and Myra to the hospital.

"Over excitement", the doctor had said of Myra's condition. "She'll be alright, there's nothing wrong with her."

For Caroline however extensive tests, scans and x rays had been carried out. "Other than a slight bruising on her left cheek and right thigh, nothing physically wrong with her either. It's basically shock because she's been through an ordeal and right now she needs to feel secure and loved. She'll be good in a couple of weeks. I've given her mild medication to calm her down. Not to worry."

The doctor had been reassuring on both counts.

To Charles' anxious expression and low voiced enquiry, the doctor had responded with a slight negative shake of his head. "There is no evidence of any other kind of abuse having taken place. So calm down and get a good night's rest. You both look like you need it" he had said nodding towards Myra.

Myra had refused to sleep however until she'd heard what had happened completely. Paula had filled her in on everything they knew.

"I can't imagine what went on in the place where they kept her. He must have frightened the child more than anything. She will have to come out of that." she said, nodding toward the sleeping child.

"So the woman, this Sarah Osborne was apparently trying to protect her. Isn't that what you're saying?"

"Looks like it. Of course we cannot rule out the possibility that she could have double crossed her husband and tried to take Caroline away for some reason of her own."

Paula had to admit the possibility.

"But somehow, I think she was trying to help her. After all she was headed this way and the guy who alerted the police said that she was trying to run from her husband while he attempted to take Caroline. The guy actually thought she was the mother."

She saw Myra's fingers involuntarily tighten their hold on Caroline.

"I think she was trying to save her" she said gently. "After all Caroline had trusted her enough to let her carry her to wherever she was planning on going. So I don't think the woman ever hurt her. She must have realized that her husband was planning to hurt her in some way and tried to escape...." her voice trailed off.

Myra nodded slowly. "I realize that. The anger and hatred I feel towards her for helping abduct my child is gone when I think of what she put herself through. She would have realized that if she were caught she would definitely die and yet she... I don't believe she did that for money or some ulterior motive. I will believe that she was trying to return Caroline to me, to us and was killed in the process."

Paula watched as she saw Myra come to terms with the realization that Sarah had intentionally or otherwise done far more for Caroline than Myra herself had ever done or ever could hope to do.

"I want to arrange a funeral for the woman to eulogize her. She has given me my life back. I feel that I owe her at least that much."

Paula nodded. "I'll see whether it could be arranged. Meanwhile take good care of the child" she said as she made her way out, with Myra's thanks ringing in her ears.

Sometimes it felt like the greatest job in the world. Like now. When she was able to bring back life into an entire family. At other times, it hurt to see the families of victims get crushed with the realization that they wouldn't be able to see their loved ones. But at least some of them get closure as opposed to the ones that lived their lives out without knowing, she thought. Not knowing is the worst feeling in the world. A person couldn't really move on unless or until they had concrete knowledge of what transpired. It would only be half a life that they were living...

Like me...

Eternal Love

Love at first sight is a myth. There are people who would make you believe that no other kind of love exists, that in the first moment you lay your eyes on that *other person,* you would feel an electric current race through your veins, shivers run down your spine and a whole lot of other strange biological phenomena manifesting themselves with alarming rapidity and making you feel dizzy. There may exist experiences like what I've just explained, I don't know, but this is something entirely different...

Samantha first met Peter at a party. She was there with a couple of her friends and Peter was celebrating his birthday. There was a lot of noise, people talking, laughing, the clinking of glasses and general air of celebration. Everything had gone better than expected and other than a slight hitch in the delivery of some food, everything went extremely well. Samantha was wearing a pale pink frock and looked ravishing. Her long brown hair was loose on her back and smelled faintly of strawberries and her eyes sparkled. Peter looked dashing in a brand new suit he'd got for the occasion. Everyone who'd come to the party commented on how great he looked. Though they saw each other, nothing clicked and they went their separate ways, he to play with his new superhero kit and she back home. Master Peter had just turned four.

❧

Peter was sent to a boys' boarding school when he turned seven. Samantha joined a prep school near her home initially and then went to St Anne's for girls. Their school years were spent in serious pursuance of their studies and they both excelled in mathematics. They never ran into each other until the first year of college. At the fresher's party organised by the seniors of the college, they met for the second time in eighteen years without realising the fact. A mutual friend introduced them to each other, mentioning that Samantha had won the 'Young mathematician award' which was the highest honour in mathematics that the school had to offer. Peter's comment to that statement was "Really? You're the first girl I've known who's got a head for Mathematics". This statement, far from flattering Samantha, made her angry. "What makes you think women are not good with numbers? Deflate that ego of yours before you speak to women!" she said, as she walked away without a backward glance. Peter looked stunned for a moment, before shrugging it off philosophically with "Women!"

But that rift didn't stay for a long time. Since both of them had exceptional mathematical aptitude, they were sent as a team to compete with other colleges in all mathematics contests. They soon became good friends and also developed into a formidable team. To Samantha's surprise she discovered that she and Peter shared a lot of common interests and even liked the same artists. He seemed like such an outdoorsy, macho kind of guy, that the idea of him having an eye for art was both intriguing as well as a little odd. Both of them spent a majority of time browsing around all the art galleries around the place. A particular little quaint gallery became a favourite haunt for both of them, especially after having faced a tough mathematical challenge. The newest painting to be delivered there depicted a man coming home. Every line of his body suggested happiness and contentment at finally reaching his destination. The expression on his face, his eyes, was tranquil. It was the most beautiful painting that had ever been displayed there. It was a personal favourite for both and they always looked with dread to see if the 'SOLD' sign was put up next to it. But it was never there.

You have received an instant message from: SAMANTHA

SAMANTHA: Hey Pete, still swallowing lessons?

PETER: Nope Sammy. Dreaming as usual. Of becoming the greatest mathematician the world has ever known.

SAMANTHA: Oh, that. Now listen to me.... John has asked me to go out on a date with him this evening.

PETER: No!

SAMANTHA: Yes! What should I do?

PETER: What do you think?

SAMANTHA: Help me out here Pete! I can't believe I'm saying this but really need your advice!

PETER: Do you want to go Sam? I can't make that decision for you.

SAMANTHA: Thanks a lot (or not)! But I guess you're right... Fine, I'm going.

SAMANTHA: What have you got to say to that?

SAMANTHA: Are you there Pete?

SAMANTHA: Hello??

SAMANTHA has logged off.

PETER: I see...

One year and Six months later Samantha's wedding took place with a lot of fanfare. Peter was the best man.

Two years later Samantha was still at home, finding it harder and harder to stay there. There was absolutely nothing to do all day. John, who had seemed so enthusiastic about her work plans before marriage had flatly refused to even listen to her after the wedding. "Why can't you be like the other women I know and try to be a good wife? Why are you always so obsessed with your career?"

"I don't have a career that's why! You wanted me to have one! You have one, why the hell shouldn't I? The one great ambition of my life and you have to put a stop to it, don't you!"

Talks turned to fights and Sam turned to Peter for help. This infuriated John even more.

"Peter this, Peter that! Talk to me, I am your husband!", but he never listened when she tried to talk.

Sam gave up trying to talk to anyone.

When she was running the dishwasher one morning, she suddenly felt a wave of nausea hit her hard and she gasped, trying to orient herself. The ground came up to meet her as she fell and she slid noiselessly to the ground.

Nine months and eleven days later, Rosie was born.

≈

Rosie's mother washed her hands tiredly. She had just finished feeding her daughter. Though her mother helped her with the baby, it was too much to ask her to do everything.

Though her life had completely changed in a way, it hadn't changed at all in others. Only now, she could never complain of having nothing to do. Having to tend to her exuberant daughter constantly, actually made her feel fatigued.

Rosie was two and a half and she was Sam's entire life. Samantha could never regret having a child but she did wish that she had a husband who would help her and support her throughout. Her back ached and her shoulders felt so sore. Tears filled her eyes as she envisaged the life she had wanted for herself, the job, the freedom and the sense of contentment she had felt sure she would achieve. Now, she couldn't bear to look at herself. Hair always tied up in a messy knot and tumbling down, dark circles under her eyes, her skin had an almost translucent texture and she'd lost weight. It was years since she had ever dressed for any occasion, now she always went around in shapeless clothes that looked worn and faded. She was twenty four and felt forty. Why did she deserve to suffer like this? No! She wouldn't think that. Never ever think that. Whatever had happened, Rosie was the only good thing that had come out of all this. The memory of seeing her daughter's face for the first time still brought tears of joy to her eyes. Just then she heard a crash. Rushing to the kitchen, she found Rosie blissfully streaking her face with some left over banana mash and cooing in delight. Heaving a sigh of combined amusement and exhaustion, Samantha moved forward to clear it up.

❧

To John Marquez, Samantha Marquez and Rosie

Jack Marshall and Rosa Marshall

proudly invite you to the marriage of their son

Peter Marshall to Rachel Keene

on July 20th of this year.

❧

Peter walked towards his office quickly. It was pretty early to be starting for work but he liked to get there early and have a little time to sort things out in peace. At twenty seven, he felt that he was reasonably successful, though his lifelong dream of becoming an honoured mathematician didn't seem to be happening at all. But he really loved his current job.

His wife was probably still sleeping. Her normal wakeup time was around ten in the morning and she proceeded at a leisurely pace to cope with the needs of the day. Since she supervised an art gallery that was owned by a close friend, she didn't have to report to work on time. She went to work at about twelve in the afternoon and skipped work altogether sometimes. Her love for art was what had attracted her to him in the first place but now he was slowly realising that it was a mistake. He knew why he had rushed into marriage with the first girl who seemed interested in him. But he couldn't think about Samantha now. What she had meant to him. What she still meant to him. Why had he talked her into marrying John? But she never thought of him, Peter, that way. That had been obvious. It was marriage she had been against, not marriage to John. In the time that he had been married to Rachel, he had realized the truth pretty quickly, that she had married him only for his money, but had refused to face it until now. He suspected that she had male friends whom he would not approve of but whenever he started to talk about them, she vehemently denied it, bursting into tears at the very mention of them. In the beginning, he had believed her and felt ashamed of himself. But lately she seemed to be less bothered about keeping up the pretence. She got on his nerves constantly and he knew that he irritated her as well. They were absolutely wrong for each other. 'How did I ever fall for her?' became a constant refrain at the back of his mind that nagged at him and made it almost impossible to think of other things sometimes. He had to put a stop to it. There was no way they could go on like this forever.

Abruptly his mind switched to Samantha. When he had seen her last, she had looked so woebegone, lost so much weight. But the look on her face, every time she glanced at Rosie... There was so much love in that glance, so much pride. It had been a long time since he called her. She mailed him every now and then but they never talked like they used to before. Pulling out his cell phone he moved to speed dial and clicked one.

The "Hello" sounded a bit hurried. Hey Sam, am I catching you at a bad time?"

"Peter!" It made his heart swell with happiness when he heard the delight in her voice. Even if he knew she was only happy at being called by her friend.

"Can I call you in fifteen minutes?" she didn't tell him John was home and would probably hit her if he knew she was talking to Peter.

"Sure" Peter assumed Rosie had to go to school and rang off.

Ten minutes and eleven seconds later the phone rang.

"Hey Sam" he responded warmly, smiling. "How is life?"

"Rosie is ten now. Can you believe it? My beautiful, wonderful baby is growing up so fast! Her best friend is Jake and the two of them hang out together practically all the time! She just loves school and I'll bet she gets to love Mathematics just as much as I do. She's going to beat every single boy in her class, you just wait!"

Peter laughed. "I see you haven't forgotten my comment yet but dream on, Rosie hates Maths, the weirdo!"

"How is Rachel, Pete?"

Peter sighed. She sounded so eager that he didn't have the heart to tell her the truth. "She's fine Sam. She's off to work now. I'll ask her to give you a call sometime." That call would never materialise. The truth was that Rachel hated Sam. In the early days of their relationship, Peter had told Rachel all about Samantha and their friendship. As a result, Rachel now flew into a temper whenever Sam was mentioned.

"Sure Pete! And..." her voice trailed off.

Peter waited expectantly. He knew Sam. There was no use rushing her. Better to wait and let her spill it out.

"I've got a job." John is not too happy about it and I got hit for even having applied for a job, she wanted to tell him but she held her tongue for two reasons. Loyalty meant a lot to her and she was a good wife, no matter what John said and she didn't want to burden Peter with her pain. Pete would come right over and give John a piece of his mind and probably a piece of action as well.

Peter gave a whoop of joy. "That's just great Sam" he said sincerely. "This is an awesome break for you and God knows you deserve it. Please talk to me more often. I miss my best friend."

He hung up still feeling elated at her happiness.

"You have one new message", the cool female voice on his answering machine informed him.

It was a week since his divorce had come through. His house felt empty, uninviting. Rachel for all her behaviour had known how to make the house feel pleasant, warm and welcoming. Now it felt cold, sterile.

"So much for being popular" he thought sarcastically as he pressed 'play'.

Sam's voice sounded low, subdued. "Just heard the news Peter. I had no idea. Call me."

So, she'd heard about his divorce. Normally he'd have been the first to tell her about his relationship with his wife, now ex wife but he hadn't had the heart to. She'd liked Rachel so much, how could he tell her that the feeling wasn't reciprocated? That his wife had only loved his wealth and not him. Somehow he couldn't.

He was still undecided on what to say as he called her.

She picked up on the second ring. He had expected her to be sad, irate, furious and even disappointed in him but not compassionate. "Tell me Pete. I don't get why you never told me before but I want to help you, be there for you like you've always been there for me. So I'll just listen."

In halting, broken sentences, he explained to her what had happened. How he had known from the start that it would never work. How he had watched his marriage fall to pieces right in front of his eyes. He nearly told her about his love, but stopped himself in time. He could never tell her. He should have told her that day in the gallery, when he had the chance. But he blew it and now would regret it for the rest of his life.

She never once interrupted him, listening to her even breathing at the other end, calmed him down, and made him more rational.

Once he finished, she talked. Telling him to think of the pleasant things, advising him now, as he had once long ago advised her.

Finally he hung up feeling much better.

You have an instant message from: SAMANTHA

SAMANTHA: Hey Pete. Things are doing ok here. Can you believe Rosie is seventeen? I cannot believe that she has grown up so fast! I feel if I blink, I'll miss some part of her life!

PETER: You and your worries! Why do you always regret her growing up so much? She is just entering the prime of life now. Let her enjoy it to the full! Trust me; she needs you to leave her in peace. Hope she got the gift I sent her and I hope that she really likes it. How is John?

SAMANTHA: Where did that come from? Has the little monkey been talking to you behind my back again? So, she needs me to 'leave her alone' does she? I'll see that I do just that!

PETER: Calm down! I'd better warn Rosie that her mother is on the warpath right now. Give it up Sam. Let her live her life. You've been a great mother to her and she will never go wrong in her choices. By the way, do they pay you at the office to chat with friends and random strangers? I'm seriously considering applying for a job there. This is your third break in two hours!

SAMANTHA: I am going back to work now, thank you very much! And Rosie is going to suffer my wrath this evening!

SAMANTHA has logged off.

❧

From: Samantha
To: Peter
Subject: Why am I alive?

Dear Pete,

I don't know if you've heard this but John and I are filing for divorce. Can you imagine? After thirty years of marriage, we've finally made the decision to split once and for all. I feel so low. He's told our marriage counsellor that we've been living a lie (at least he has) and that I am a horrible wife. He says that I am never there for him and that he's suffered in silence for twenty years. I think he almost hates me. I knew he didn't like you because you were my best friend. And... I never told you this before, but he hit me Pete. Every day. Every single day. It was living hell. Rosie was the only one that kept me sane and she is happy that this decision has been made. It took a lot of courage for her to tell me that. Like me she has that fierce streak of loyalty. She thought she wasn't being loyal to her dad if she sided with me. How many nights, that child has cried herself to sleep over our tantrums you wouldn't believe if I told you. The fact that she sides with me and not her father infuriated him. He almost hit her too, when she was home on a break from the hospital. I was thrilled at the thought of the reunion with my daughter but this happened. That decided me. No way in hell was I going to let my daughter suffer like me! I filed for a divorce then.

I feel so tired Pete. Like I don't want to live anymore. Seems like all my life has been a lie. Call me when you can.

Bye,
A very miserable Sam.

Two minutes later...

"Yeah, Pete?" Sam's voice was subdued, reflecting her pain.

"Sam, I just don't know what to say. I'm really sorry. But why didn't you ever tell me before? I am your best friend and always have been. How could you have put up with that all these years and not said a word?! That cheap shot was absolutely wrong for you and we both know it. It was a miracle that the marriage lasted as long as it did. I know what you had to put up with Sam. He never deserved you."

"Now you tell me! Both you and Rosie simply drive me up the wall! Why couldn't you have told me sooner how this would end up? I wouldn't have been saddled with all this wasted grief and pain. But then you never knew..." Sam's voice broke at the last word.

"Sammy, Sammy, don't cry. Sammy darling, please don't cry."

A long pause ensued. Both sides were silent.

Then, "What? What did you just call me?"

A pause and then "it came out unintentionally but I am not going to hold it back any longer. I've waited long enough. You are a fifty year old woman and I am a fifty one year old man. By all rights, we are too old for this. But I am not ashamed to say I love you. I have loved you since the day I saw you at the art gallery when you told me that you didn't want marriage. I love you with all my heart."

A startled gasp and a longer pause and then "Peter Marshall! Are you listening to yourself?!"

"You bet I am Sam! I am finally saying it! I should have said it long ago. I have been a fool, a complete fool!"

Samantha took a deep breath, "Why on earth would you have told me to marry John, you!" Suddenly she was shouting "Oh Peter why did you never tell me this before?"

Now it was his turn to be amazed. "You mean?"

"I loved you too. I hoped that you would stop me and tell me you loved me when I told you about John. I was waiting for you to do that. But you never did. And later you seemed happy with my decision. I just assumed, you didn't want me" Sam's voice was almost a whisper.

Peter could feel tears in his eyes. "Oh Sam... I am not saying another word over the phone. I am starting there right now and I'll be there in four hours. Remember that picture in the gallery that we used to go to? The picture that we both used to stare at for hours on end. We both loved it the best. That is how I feel now. I can at long last understand what the artist meant when he painted that picture. I am coming home Sam. Finally...to you, my love."

Samantha hung up in a daze.

It was him; finally it was him, the man who had at last told her what she meant to him and was coming to see her.

She had loved him since the first moment she had met him. He had always been there for her. She thought of the picture he'd talked about. She wondered if it was still there in the gallery. Not likely. Not after so many years. But it wouldn't do any harm to check. If it was there, it would be the best homecoming gift to Peter.

She drove the ten miles to the store. And miracle of miracles, the picture still hung there in its same spot, unchanged and still beautiful. Staring at it Sam felt sudden moisture spring to her eyes and she wept unashamedly. The manager hurriedly looked the other way, flustered. She didn't care. This was her moment. Finally, her moment had come.

Clutching the paper wrapped painting in her hand and walking over to her car, she reflected that life had finally decided to reward her now.

Back home, she decided that she would let Peter choose the spot where the painting would be hung. All those conversations with him, every award they'd won together, all the fun they'd had in college, the art galleries they visited, the beautiful silences they'd shared when words were superfluous, she remembered everything like it was just yesterday.

In a nervous burst of energy, she cleaned the house and threw the windows wide open. Peter loved fresh air. A cool breeze wafted in. She had moved to her parents' house the day she filed for a divorce and though they weren't here anymore, she could feel them watching over her, sharing her happiness and sense of contentment that was hers at last. All those years of silent suffering, never daring to tell anyone, even her parents, all that was behind her. She was free.

Four hours and forty five minutes later…

The phone rang just as she thought she heard the front door bell.

Habit made her pick up the phone first.

"Mrs. Samantha Marquez?" it was an unfamiliar voice.

"Yes, it is I", she answered suddenly feeling a pang of fear.

"Do you know a Mr. Peter Marshall?"

"Yes" her voice caught in her throat making it almost impossible to speak.

"We regret to inform you ma'am, that there has been an accident…"

A RANDOM ACT
OF KINDNESS

I enjoyed a brief stint as a kindergarten teacher. It was one of the things I'd always wanted to do and when I decided that I'd had enough of being a software programmer, I quit and took up a position as KG teacher in a local school. It was everything I dreamed it would be, a paltry salary, screaming kids, parents showing up at all hours to complain about the management, paper corrections like you wouldn't believe and a tyrannical headmaster whom I feared more than my students did. Don't get me wrong, corporate life was exacting in its own way, with short deadlines, being online practically the whole day and cut- throat competition. But kindergarten was mayhem compared to that. Every night I would come home, dog-tired and longing for a hot shower and sleep and the next morning I'd be in tears at the thought of going back to school.

After a few weeks I noticed that one teacher in particular never seemed to be frazzled by all that was going on around him. He was nicknamed 'The Saint' and after a few days I knew why. He had the record of being the only teacher who never punished his students no matter what they did. Every teacher in the place had asked him the secret to his patience and he'd smile and say "Kindness". They all just shook their heads at him in wonderment and went on their way, accepting if not understanding that there was something special about him.

It was not just that he didn't punish students; he never raised his voice when objecting to anything, he always had a kind word for everyone. I noticed that when we had gone on a tour to the local museum and were returning, he was the only person who thought of offering tea and biscuits to the bus driver. He took the little helper boy who worked at school along with the students whenever we went on field trips, telling the headmaster in his gentle voice that even if he couldn't afford to give the boy regular education, these short trips would not only give him an informal education but also be a well deserved break for the child.

Not surprisingly all the kids loved him and willingly worked hard for the subjects he taught. On a rainy Tuesday, I had a free hour after lunch (heaven!) and decided to spend it napping in the staff room which would probably be empty. When I made my way over to the staff room however, I found the Saint sitting serenely correcting math homework notebooks. All thoughts of sleep vanished and I took a seat next to him. Ever the gentleman, he put down his work and turned to me with a smile. "What can I do for you?" he asked me.

Smiling back, I asked him "What is your secret?" I went on "I really want to know what has made you who you are today. Please don't just say kindness and leave it at that. There has to be something, some incident that made you see what kind of person you wanted to be in your life."

He looked at me curiously for a moment or two before speaking. "The way you phrased your question… It sounded almost like you knew" he paused and then went on "there was an incident which was the turning point in my life. That is completely true, yes. Before that I was very much like everyone else, going through life without any deep thought as to what I was doing or why I was doing it."

I settled myself in an attitude of deep listening. I got the feeling that something truly profound was going to be said.

"I was working in an insurance company before I took up teaching as my profession."

I was about to interrupt, saying that I had worked as a corporate professional before this too, when I caught sight of his face. I sensed that he was in earnest and I automatically closed my mouth. I did not want to interrupt his thoughts. He glanced at me with a half smile as though sensing that I had been about to say something and was silent for a few moments waiting for me to speak, out of politeness. When I said nothing, he continued:

"A friend of mine was widely involved in charitable activities. He provided generous funding to many charitable trusts and institutions and sponsored education for a lot of under privileged children. We had been friends for many years and while I applauded his efforts, I never thought to take a more active interest in what he was doing. Don't ask me why… I just never thought enough about anything then. I wanted to live well and that was all I cared about. In a way I feel that I was worse than anyone who felt anger or hatred. Because anger and hatred are strong emotions and to feel them, some part of you must care. What I felt, on the other hand, was indifference. This meant I didn't have enough emotion to care."

I waited, uncomfortably aware that he had just described what was unarguably my state of mind as well. Not bothering enough to care...

He glanced at me as though aware of what I was thinking. "Don't beat yourself up about it. But do change while you can... As I was saying:"

"One day my friend showed up at my door, determined to make me see sense. I humored him, thinking then in my short sighted way, that if he became really insistent, I would maybe make out a cheque for a sizeable amount and he would be satisfied at that. I didn't know then that money, while it could do a lot of good when used in the right way, was only a tool. An act of kindness is the most important requirement when it came to doing good for others.

He started without any preliminary small talk. He said that it worried him that I thought money was the most important aspect of a good life.

I had to see, he said what it was like to not have opportunities in life. People suffered so much and were in need of concern and help from others. I thought to myself that he was taking things too seriously. I watched the news every day and was quite aware of the horrors happening in the world. So? There was nothing I could do about it. I had my own life to think of and I didn't see why he was making such a big deal of it. He continued talking for quite some time.

I was only half listening. My mind was more occupied with analyzing the market demand for shares in an official presentation that was due the next day. I was still grappling with the problem when he stopped talking. Realizing belatedly that I had let quite some time pass before I understood that he had become silent, I was still bobbing my head at intervals to give him the impression that I was listening attentively.

I stopped and gave him a sheepish grin. I repeatedly said I was sorry, asking him to forgive me. I even presented him with a cheque which I thought would appease his mind. He became so incensed that he tore the cheque in half. That was when I realized how serious he was about the whole thing. He was angry and then finally he was sad. "You are my best friend" he said "and it saddens me to think that after all this time I haven't been able to get through to you at all."

I felt very ashamed that I had hurt my friend so deeply. More to calm him down than anything else, I asked him what he wanted me to do.

He gave me a most surprising reply. He told me that there was an orphanage for children and elders that he knew of and that he wanted me to go and stay there for ten days. No cell phones, laptops or any office equipment. I was to forget everything and go and stay at that place taking only the bare necessities.

Ten whole days of being off the grid, unavailable for contact. I was to take no books and nothing to amuse myself with. I was to practically live the life of an orphan in those ten days and if at the end of those ten days, if I still felt the same way, then he would say no more about it. I could do as I pleased and he wouldn't interfere at all.

I started to protest but he held my hand and told me that this was the one thing he asked for from me in this entire lifetime.

Seeing how earnest he was, I came to a decision. I told him I needed a couple of days to set my affairs in order and then I would do as he asked. Satisfied, he left me to complete my presentation in peace.

After two days, I set off to the orphanage thinking in my mind that it was a kind of vacation. I needed the break anyway, I was too focused on the office. The orphanage turned out to be a tiny place with no ventilation. As soon as I entered, I began hastily rethinking my decision to stay here. It looked too crowded as it was and it didn't look like they could accommodate anyone else. Then I remembered that it was not my decision but that of my friend.

Sighing, I went and unpacked my suitcase and put my belongings in the tiny shelf that was apparently my wardrobe. Everything in this place was communal and there were no separate quarters for anybody. I shared my shelf with two little children and one old lady. But their welcome was warm. Despite the cramped quarters they looked at me like they were really happy to have me join their little group.

Men slept in the hallway and women and children had the inner room for themselves. There were no beds. Flat mattresses which provided no lumbar support were spread on the floor and covered every inch of it. Everybody had to lie down in them next to one another like fish on a slab. One man saw me eyeing the setup apprehensively. I'd always liked having a lot of room to move around when I slept. He laughed and told me that we were lucky. Some of the children in the other room had the habit of violently kicking the person lying next to them. We didn't have to deal with that. Put that way, it certainly seemed that luck had favored me.

I had reached the place after lunch time and the old people were getting ready to nap. I decided to read a while but then realized that I had no books with me. I didn't feel like lying down in the middle of the day. If I had been in the office, I would have been immersed in tracking the volatility of the market and would probably have been yelling at some unlucky chap at the office on selling or buying shares, depending on whether the market was bullish or bearish.

I decided to have a little stroll around the place. After all, if I was going to be stuck here for ten days, I might as well get the hang of what was happening. That was my rule of life, preparation and planning. I never had been impulsive before. Not even when I was a young boy. I had always preferred to familiarize myself with what I was about to deal with. Phrases like 'winging it', 'playing it by ear' and 'going with the flow' were alien concepts that I didn't even attempt to fathom.

I made my way out of the little building, nodding to the lady in charge, who looked ready for a nap herself and into what could be, at a stretch, called the garden. It was unkempt with grass and weeds growing everywhere and dandelions swaying gently in the breeze. It was quite hot, with the sun shining fiercely down but there was a soft little wind as well, reassuringly blowing along and trying to make people feel cooler. There were a couple of mango trees and I could see small mangoes already starting to form in them. As I looked on, I wondered when was the last time I had actually looked at nature and seen the beauty in it. Our house did have a garden of sorts and it was tended to by a gardener who came twice weekly, but I never had the time to admire his handiwork.

A couple of children were playing on the ground next to me and some other bigger children were playing a little farther away. As I watched, one of the bigger boys yelled and pointed to the tree. The others also looked on as he lithely swung himself on to the first branch. Soon everyone was swarming up the tree. The one who started first was near the top and happily plucking the mangoes which were still mostly raw. He threw one to everyone below him and then catching sight of me, threw one to me as well. I fumbled the catch and it fell to the ground. I could hear the kids laughing and I felt stupid as I leaned down and picked it up. But as I straightened up, I saw that they were not jeering at me but simply laughing in the spirit of fun. I could feel my face break into a smile as I took in the happy faces, grinning at me from the tree. Suddenly I felt young again…

After having worked for years at an office where everyone's sole happiness was to watch you crash and burn, I remembered how hard it had been to stay on top of my game and cement my position in the firm. There was practically no laughter there and if there was, it was certainly not the good natured kind. I went back into the building feeling better than I had, in years.

The next day was more eventful for me, as I embarked on gardening. In the ten days that I stayed here, I would do something nice like clearing up the weeds and cutting the grass. I found some old gardening tools in the back yard which were covered with rust but I had to make do with them. It was definitely tough going. But some of the bigger boys, seeing me wrestle with the weeds came over to help me and from then on, it became easier. I noticed that I didn't have to keep calling them to help me or demanding that they do work. They saw me working and simply jumped right in, another aspect that was missing in the corporate culture.

The days went by and the garden was beginning to live up to its name. I felt nice here but no great feeling of social responsibility overwhelmed me. Everyone here was very pleasant and so was I. I could see that there was no luxury here but I had settled in just fine and I could see that they managed too, as well. My friend was evidently seeing to it that they didn't starve and it seemed that, that was all they wanted. And quite frankly I thought that once this simple living ended for them, they would become obnoxious like most of the urban population.

I grew particularly fond of watching two young children play. One was a boy who was about five and the other was a three and a half year old girl and they seemed inseparable. They had their meals together and spent the rest of the time playing little games of their own invention. They never seemed to play the same game twice. On the third day of my stay, a small dog wandered into the garden and these two at once took him under their wing. They dragged him over to where they were playing and took turns trying to fit him into a little mud house they had built. As a result the house collapsed on the dog before it got in and in the ensuing melee, the puppy shook himself thoroughly covering the two of them with mud from top to toe. After that the puppy became their shared pet and it stayed on quite happily.

The next day they seemed to want to play houses and spent the whole afternoon pretending to take care of the little mud house which they had re erected after much work. The house was still very shaky but they played with it quite happily. The little girl went around picking random flowers from little shrubs in the garden and the boy went around picking up pebbles that struck his fancy. They seemed to consider these the most important commodities to run a house properly.

The little girl always saved any sweet or chocolate that was given and gave it to the boy at once. She seemed to have no desire to eat them herself. The others just smilingly shook their heads as they watched them.

On the seventh day of my stay the puppy went missing. We searched all over the place but no matter how hard we tried, we couldn't find him anywhere. We concluded that he had run off outside and that there was no point in looking for him anymore. The small boy was inconsolable. He refused to eat or play. The little girl must have also been upset about the dog but she was more concerned about her best friend. She tried to get him to eat but he adamantly refused, bursting into tears when anyone attempted to force him. Eventually we all gave up and went on to do other work. That evening there was a huge storm with a heavy downpour of rain. Thunder and lightning split the sky and almost deafened everyone. Predictably, the electricity went off and we were stuck in darkness, hearing the thunder roar while brief snatches of lightning broke the otherwise complete darkness. The rain didn't look like it would ever stop and we slowly went off to bed one by one finding that there wasn't anything better to do.

I finally lay down thinking that there was no way I'd be able to sleep with all the noise the thunder was making. Surprisingly I slept quite soon that night and didn't wake till about six in the morning. The sound of a crowing rooster from somewhere far away, woke me up from the depths of my sleep.

Everyone around me was slowly stirring awake and some of the women were already awake and talking in low voices. As I got up, one of them came up to me, looking very worried. She told me that she couldn't find the little girl. She had woken up around five, she said and had not been able to find the child. I tried not to panic as I thought about what to do. It was still quite early and I couldn't think where she could have gone. I finally decided to round up a small search party and look for her before taking any drastic decision. It would look very stupid if the child was playing somewhere nearby and we panicked and called the police.

We rounded up some members and started going around, calling her name. The rain had still not ceased but it was not pouring like the night before. It had slowed to a steady drizzle and I squinted, trying to look around. We first checked the garden thoroughly and it was evident she was not there. We started down the road then, each of us going in a different direction and calling out. I could feel the panic in me begin to rise. The child was just three and she couldn't have wandered far.

As if to prove me right, I was the one that found her first. When I turned the next corner, I almost fell into a ditch and that was where I caught a wisp of white fabric, wet with rain and half immersed in the mud. My voice sounded strange to my own ears as I screamed hoarsely out, calling to everyone else to come and help me. I leaped into the ditch and cleared away some debris which was the result of the rain last night. I picked up the tiny unmoving body, refusing to accept what had happened. "No, no no" I mouthed hoarsely as I felt for her pulse and found nothing. There was a big gash on her hairline where it had hit on a sharp rock. I felt my breath catch in my chest as I saw the front of her dress move slightly. She was holding something tightly in her hands. It was the little dog that had run away yesterday and she had found it just like she had promised her friend. She must have wandered here in the dead of the night in pouring rain, to try to find the dog when the rest of us were sleeping like logs. I had almost fallen into the ditch in broad daylight and in the dead of the night, with the rain pouring down, she never had a chance…"

The Saint looked up at me, tears shining in his eyes. I felt dimly how wet my own cheeks were. His voice was shaky and I could feel him reliving the entire episode again. He continued: "that was when I realized, that giving was much greater than receiving. A three year old child taught me that and to this day, I thank her for it."

I simply nodded at him numbly. Words seemed superfluous. I was aware of the sounds around me but they seemed to be coming from far away, everyday noises that filled the school corridors. Suddenly I became aware that someone was addressing me.

A small child from my class obediently stood in attention next to me. "Ma'am, it is your class now ma'am. Will you be coming now?"

I nodded as I got up and told her to go back to class. It had stopped raining and the sun was shining brightly from the window. I noticed how the leaves of plants in the little portico outside gleamed with raindrops. The smell of wet earth mingled with the sweet scent of flowers filled the open corridor as I walked towards my class.

A small act of kindness had had such a huge impact in the lives of everyone around. The term 'butterfly effect' suddenly struck me and for the first time I wondered if it didn't just refer to a scientific phenomenon. Could it also refer to acts of kindness? Was it Mother Teresa who said "The words of kindness may be small but their echoes are truly endless…"?

I told you that I had a brief stint as a Kindergarten teacher. That was completely true. I found that I could do better after all. Both The Saint and I run the orphanage together now. We have plans of improving the infrastructure and taking in as many people as we can. We have convinced the headmaster of our school(the one I so feared) to allow the children to visit the orphanage once a month to help them develop an awareness of the lives of others and to instill in them a willingness to help and be kind to people and animals. The members of our orphanage, I need hardly say, look forward to these visits very much.

Be the change you so wish to see…….

THE DAY AFTER TOMORROW

I had a very happy childhood. At the risk of sounding clichéd, I choose to begin my story like this because it's entirely true. I was loved by my parents and friends and I am told that I was worth all the attention. I was a polite child, respectful to a fault, never throwing tantrums or behaving like a spoilt child. Well, almost never. Of course, I wasn't perfect and occasionally did have a few spells of disobedience, but nothing major. Everyone always remarked to my parents that I was such a pet and that they'd brought me up well. I liked to look at my parents' faces when someone complimented me, their proud smiles and sparkling eyes were like elixir to my existence. In a nutshell, I lived to please.

And then I became five. I had been healthy since the time I was born and except for the occasional bouts of cold, I was pretty robust. So you can imagine my parents' shock, dismay and fear when I was diagnosed with childhood leukaemia. At that point, I didn't even grasp the significance of the fact that I had one of the most dreaded diseases on earth. It started out simply enough. I had gone to the hospital for what my parents thought was a simple ailment.

The doctor however was convinced that it wasn't quite that simple and immediately ordered a barrage of tests at the end of which it was pretty evident that I had the dreaded illness.

My parents were devastated. Naturally in a world where the mortality rate of carcinoma far exceeded the rate of patients who made it out alive, they practically equated cancer to death. I vaguely remembered my mother sobbing for hours, days, weeks while my dad tried to comfort her without breaking down himself. A lot should be said of my father. He was like a rock, my pillar of support and my mother's only comfort. I know the agony of what he must have gone through, his only daughter hovering on the brink of death. But he fought against my disease with as much spirit as David in his fight with Goliath. That particular story has always appealed to me the most, perhaps because of its significance to the way my life was then.

Without being aware of it, I was brave. My dad helped me by trying to make the visits to the hospitals fun. Any person who's ever been in one will realise that that battle would be lost before it even began. Nevertheless, he struggled to make me feel good about it. Perhaps that would account for the fact that till date I don't fear hospitals at all. And given the harrowing time I had, the tortures of therapy that I went through, this is an achievement to be proud of and I salute my father for achieving the impossible. Of all the treatments that I had, I hated chemotherapy the worst. When I was diagnosed, I was somewhere in the middle of the primary and secondary stages. They tried to initially cure me without subjecting me to surgery. Chemotherapy made my hair fall out and I went about looking like a weirdo. People tried hard not to stare at me but that very act showed me what a freak I was and how much they pitied me for it. But it was hopeless and as the cancer quickly progressed, they finally started having talks with my parents about surgical procedures.

The thought of having to go under the knife was not daunting to me at all. Except for a vague foreboding, I confess I was actually excited about it. But my mother was inconsolable. According to her I was going to die anyways and making me undergo surgery was simply speeding up the process. This attitude hurt me a little. As I said I hadn't quite understood the magnitude of the situation and death didn't mean anything to me at all. In some level, I felt my mother moving away from me, preparing for a life without me. In hindsight, I now understand that it's basically a survival instinct and am able to forgive my mother. But at that point of time, I was pretty upset and complained often to my father. That saint of a man of course had an explanation for my mom's irrational behaviour, her wild love for me at times and bouts of depression at others where I felt like she'd built a wall around herself which I couldn't intrude.

So finally I was going in for surgery! I told all my friends about it and wondered why they didn't respond with the enthusiasm I hoped they would display on my behalf. There were a few as clueless as I who thought it was all pretty exciting but most of them acted sad. They had a lot of maturity even then and it surprises me to this day that they displayed a maturity far beyond their years. My mom packed a few of my clothes in a small case and we set off for the hospital, tears silently coursing through my mother's cheeks. By then I was used to it and instead concentrated on putting my head out the window and looking at the scenic wonders as we whizzed past.

A glance inside the car showed that even my dad was unusually silent and brooding, afraid to speak and display any emotion that would frighten me. At the hospital I grew a little worried as I saw the nurses and doctors walk around me talking in hushed whispers and twiddling knobs on some weird machine that they hooked up to me. Since I had a healthy heart, the anaesthesia was administered quickly and I went under without a hitch. Of course, I don't remember anything about the actual surgery. If I did I probably wouldn't be alive today. Once it was completed, I was kept under observation for a few days and then finally discharged.

I wasn't able to resume my activities of erstwhile for quite some time, and that made me mad. I had hoped to return bounding with happiness and brimming with energy to my former life, but the surgery had taken its toll and I remember that sometimes even I felt tired and fatigued. However my parents were happy that I'd made it through the surgery alive that I was showered with gifts and love to the point of spoiling me. My mother was close to me again and my dad was the happiest he'd been in a year. This was a very pleasant state of affairs and helped lift some of the vacillating aimlessness I felt. If you are wondering at my accurate recall of the earlier stages of my life, let me make things clear by saying that I have what is known as an eidetic memory and that I remember every single thing whether I want to or not. Not to mention that my parents need no reminding of what they went through and helped me out when I got stuck.

A few months later I was taken to the hospital again to check my condition. The doctor went through the usual motions of ordering the battery of tests and looking over what showed up in them. The cancer had significantly reduced but was by no means completely gone. I would have to go under the knife again and then maybe I would be free of this forever. My mother literally fainted and my dad looked like he very much wanted to. The problem of being a man and having to be the strength of the family was something that was a hard thing to do under normal circumstances and he couldn't afford the little luxuries like weeping endlessly and practically doing nothing of value. My dad felt that he was frankly unequal to the task but rallied his forces with a strength born of desperation as he listened, as the doctor took him through the medical rigmarole again.

So the whole sequence of things was repeated again with me being more stoic and resigned rather than excited. After it was done I went home and sulked. This ruddy thing was taking a lot more time than I had anticipated and had a few little extra pains thrown in starting with me losing my hair. My parents were kind, patient and understanding despite the fact that they were going through a lot more trauma than I was. As the aggrieved survivor, I made it a point to milk the whole thing for all it was worth and got a lot more stuff than I deserved.

The final much dreaded check up was done and the tests showed up absolutely no signs of cancer. I was rid of it at last and owe it all to my father. I often wonder how he managed to get through the ordeal.

Now that I am an oncologist, I definitely have to ask him......